Flight of the Maita
Book one
Flight of the Maita

Introducing the continuing character.

<u>Critic comment</u>
Perhaps a bit juvenile in parts, but surprisingly readable. While no great literary work, it is more than worth the price. – P.A. **½

While I was unimpressed with Moulton's style, I found the story better than average. I thought, when they were first introduced, that the use of brackets and asterisks would detract, then grew to very much like the device. It separates the characters quite nicely, and Moulton does not over-use them. If they remain as character indications for no more than the two or three principal characters, it will be successful. – GLB – Recommended

Flight of the Maita
Book one
Flight of the Maita
© 1985, 2012 & 2016 by C. D. Moulton

The abduction and overthrow of the Pweetoos, and the introduction of main continuing characters.

Contents

About the author

CD was born in Lakeland, Florida, in 1938. He is educated in genetics and botany. He has traveled over much of the world, particularly when he was in music as a rock rhythm guitarist with some well-known bands in the late sixties and early seventies. He has worked as a high steel worker and as a longshoreman, clerk, orchidist, bar owner, salvage yard manager and landscaper – among other things.

CD began writing fiction in 1984 and has more than 300 books published as of 3/15/16 in SciFi, murder, orchid culture and various other fields.

He now resides in Puerto Armuelles, David and Gualaca, Chiriqui, Panamá, where he continues research into epiphytic plants and plays music with friends. He loves the culture of the indigenous people and counts a majority of his closer friends among that group. Several have "adopted" him as their father. He funds those he can afford through the universities where they have all excelled. "The Indios are very intelligent people, they are simply too poor (in material things and money. Culturally, they are very wealthy) to pursue higher education." CD loves Panamá and the people, despite horrendous experiences (Free e-book; *Fading Paradise*). He plans to spend the rest of his life in the paradise that is Panamá

- Estrelita Suarez V. de Jaramillo – 3/15/2016

CD is the discoverer of the Chadam Protocol for the curing of cancer.

Facebook page Ambrosia peruviana for cancer

Flight of the Maita
Book one
Prologue to the Series

The intention today is to write about ten books, including some of short stories – but I tend to get into things. If the interest is there I will, no doubt, write more.

That will depend on my own interest in the characters and the forms as well as on input from friends who read the things. If I get enough encouragement I will write on.

The stories will be written for a select audience of people who like the "Star Wars" type of thing with bigger-than-life heroes and characters who have flaws, but who rise above those imperfections to be something more than they were. There will be not be gratuitous vulgarity, violence, sex – or anything else, except my own weird imagination.

If anyone is looking for what today passes for "Passion" or "Action" or "Modern themes and terms" or such, watch TV. There's no shortage of that crap there.

Our story opens with our hero, or one of them, in any case, on the beach near Midnight Pass (There once was such a pass, but a storm filled it in) in Sarasota, Florida, on a relatively comfortable night in late September, 1985. He is with several people he met that day and some girls they had picked up in a shopping center. They are very typical people of the time.

Steve Zutec, soon to be known as simply "Z", is using one of his lines on a girl, which includes acting miffed at her and deserting the group to walk along the beach for a distance, then to return all apologies for being such an ass, at which time she is expected to fall into his arms. This particular pickup line hasn't ever quite worked, but hope springs eternal.

As he approaches the pass he sees something in the water.

Z is 26 years old, athletic but slender build, thick brown hair and brown eyes. He is of average looks, though his sense of humor and charm are sensed immediately when one meets him. He is a bit shy and inhibited, but is quite likeable. Cats, dogs and children are drawn to him.

There is in the same galaxy, the one we call the Milky Way, a small (relatively) empire that consists of a few worlds that are under the domination of a race of insectoid beings known as the Pweetoos. They are totally emotionless beings who treat those under their rule anything but well, though it isn't a deliberate thing. They act from a strange logic that contains neither actual compassion nor deliberate cruelty.

Not conscious cruelty. Their cruelty is extreme, but is not deliberate.

The empire has become stagnated. Advance among insectoids is excessively slow. They are planning to expand their sphere of influence and are acting in accordance with their own strange logic. They are seeking other types of beings who are far better equipped to advance science, so are seeking among emerging cultures for any who may have the ability to aid them.

Thus are Z and his companions kidnapped and thus does he find himself setting out on an adventure unequaled in all the history of the galaxy. He will meet many peoples of many types from many wildly differing cultures, but he will learn some basic truths about those peoples.

There is a companion Z will meet on that slave ship who is the very last one he would believe would become his closest friend for the next few hundred years. Which one that is shall be left to the later stories. Z will have a few close friends, some of surprising aspect. He will confound and confuse them for a long time with his sense of humor. That sense of fun will change those he becomes closest to in ways yet to be divulged. He will also learn much from them.

And then there's the ship. There are some surprises there, too!

The friends and adventurers will eventually form a core of four radically different beings who share some most important qualities. Who those four are will not be revealed for almost two hundred years. (If the series continues. I have a few ideas about it.) We do know Z is one, but how many others are on this first trip?

And is Z, therefore all the people of Earth, of the lost race of the Maita?

C. D. Moulton – September 29, 1985

Flight of the Maita

Rude Awakening

Steven Parker "Zoot" Zutec awakened in some mildly confused discomfort, caused mostly by the thin rope that passed beneath him across the hard metal floor.

Rope?

Hard metal floor?

His first thought was, "I can't be drunk! I haven't had more than a beer in over two years!"

He looked up and into a pair of very dark eyes set into a brown furry face. The face was on a creature who was huddled into the corner to his right and across from him. It appeared to be trying to press itself into the hard metal of the wall. The little fellow was obviously terrified!

What was all this? Had he been hurt in some way that he was now hallucinating? Was this some sort of weird hospital? A hospital that tied patients with ropes around their waists?

Get serious!

It could be a dream. Some of them started like this and he'd had dreams before where he knew he was dreaming.

He looked back to the animal – guy? There seemed to be intelligence in those eyes, though Zoot wasn't the best judge of that. He estimated it would stand four feet tall if it were standing.

To his left of that being and directly across from him was a little squarish rubbery-looking thing with four tentacles in lieu of arms and legs. It had eyes on short stalks and sat back, meeting his gaze without blinking with one eye, while the other looked to his left.

Now *that* was some imagination! It was also more than just a bit creepy.

Farther along that smooth wall was a rectangular recess for an opening. The door had no handles, grooves, knobs or other features or projections. He felt it was a sliding door and would be electrically operated.

Oh, great! Analyze how a door works in a dream!

Standing on the other side of the door panel on that wall was another furry creature, also about four feet tall. It was thinner than the first and had the largest, shiniest eyes Zoot had ever seen. The long fingers and toes were widely splayed on the tips. It seemed more puzzled than afraid, and met his gaze without blinking.

Naw! This couldn't be a dream!

Zoot began to know a bit of a gnawing fear, but his good humor came to the forefront. Those guys had slipped him some acid! He should know by now you can't trust people you meet on vacation at the beach! That had to be it!

It was funny, in an odd way. Zoot had never used any drugs, except pot, a couple of times, and didn't particularly like that. He was the type who wanted to be in control of himself at all times.

This wasn't so bad. It certainly *seemed* real enough!

Past the corner and to the left was what appeared to be a rather large powerfully built Panda bear. It was coal black and paper white in patches and glared about it at all it saw.

What would make him see something like that? Was it Frank, who all the girls described as a big, lovable Teddy Bear of a guy?

That one wasn't very lovable-looking!

The rest of that wall was a featureless blank, except for several very slightly recessed areas. Those areas had small colored lights in rows along one side. The wall from the corner was slightly curved and there was nothing from the corner to Zoot.

When Zoot turned to his right, he did a double-take. The last member of the group was a Wooky!

"Jeez! You look almost like Chewbacca in the old Star Wars movie!" he exclaimed. "All right, now. Either I'm dreaming, I'm hallucinating, this is some kind of overly-elaborate joke, or it's real. I'm not really too wild about any of those options, at this point!"

He swung his foot at the wall. It clanged and hurt like all hell.

"I'm not asleep."

He shook his head from side to side, then up and down, and finished by striking the side of his head sharply with the heel of his hand.

"Guhh! Oww!"

The only result was a sharp increase in the intensity of his headache. The way the others were looking at him made him feel foolish.

Oh, well!

"I'm not hallucinating. At least, I don't think so."

He studied the tentacled being for a few moments. It was now swaying back and forth on the lower tentacles and looking around the room in several directions at once. Its eyes, rather obviously, worked independently.

"There ain't no way that can be faked! Not that good, it can't!

"That leaves me with the scariest explanation of all. I'm – I mean *we're* – really here!" He looked thoughtful. "Only, where is 'here'?"

He noticed they were all tied to rings set into the walls. The rope around his waist was what had awakened him. It was a very smooth shiny white nylon-like material in general appearance, approximately one-half inch gauge, and cast in one piece. The loop around his waist was snug, but not really too uncomfortable. It went from there to the ring in the wall and through the metal loop. It fit closely against the metal of the ring. It didn't have any knots or connectors, and seemed to be one flowing piece.

He took a grip on the rope and yanked. No give. He jerked, twisted, pulled and tried anything else that he could think of. It was far too strong.

He stood to inspect the attachment ring. It was smooth metal, three quarters of an inch thick and about four inches in diameter. It was cast into the wall. He pulled and yanked, but had no hope the ring would give.

He put his finger through the ring and shook and pulled. Nothing.

As he stood with his finger through the ring, he felt a slight vibration in the wall. He looked around the room again to find the whole group watching him. The Panda made sounds that sounded like guttural Russian to him.

"Hey! That's an idea!" he exclaimed. "Does anyone here understand English?"

They stared at him.

"Habla Español?"

Nothing. He wished he'd taken a language or two in school. This probably wouldn't work, but he wouldn't feel quite so silly.

"Parley voo French?"

Still nothing.

"Sayonara?"

The Wooky made a sound somewhere between a growl and a chuckle.

"I can't help it! Every time I look at you I think of a Wooky! How about if I call you Ape, OK? – At least, until I find out what your real name is. I'll have to be able to call you something. I can't think if I don't have the label."

He looked at the Panda-like being. "I'll call you Bear." That got a deep growl. Surly fellow.

He studied the next one. "You, I'll call ET. You remind me of another old movie, somehow – I've got it! Those wide tips on your fingers! You, I'll call ET."

The next one stopped him cold. "I don't know what to

call an octopus – or quadropus, as the case may be. I'll just call you Thing.

"And you're Joe!" he said to the being crouched against the wall. "There was an old comic strip character who went around with a cloud over his head that kept dripping on him. He was Joe Something. For some reason, you seem like the kind of guy life just keeps kicking hell out of. You're Joe."

He pointed at each as he repeated their names. "So you'll be Bear, you're ET, you're Thing, Joe and Ape.

"Just call me 'Z'. It's a lot easier than Zoot – and I never liked Zoot, anyhow.

"So, somebody else say something. Tell me to piss the hell off. Anything? We've got to communicate!"

He looked at each of them, but got no response, except from Ape, who put his hands palm upward and shrugged.

"At least you know what in the hell I'm trying to do," he muttered. "Say! I'll go to the end of my rope – my, how very fitting! – and you come to meet me."

Z went as close to Ape as the rope would permit. He waved for Ape to come toward him and reached as far as his arm would allow toward the being. It reached back. Their fingers were about six inches apart.

"At least we know. I can't reach you and you can't reach me. Maybe that's best. You're big enough to break me in half with one swipe."

There was a click and a buzz from the far end of the room. After about ten seconds the door slid upward and a totally new type of being entered. Z no longer considered whether or not this was real. It was.

Now, he must decide what was going on, where he was, how he got there – and how to get back out. Anything may be important. Anything at all.

OK. There was some warning, if ever it was needed. That door took ten seconds to open and slid upward into the wall. He looked carefully at the strange nightmare thing that entered – well, maybe not that bad. It was about five feet tall and was composed of four distinct segments. The segments were roughly spherical and were placed one atop the other. The lower three were about the same size, while the one on top was smaller. The lower segment had two legs, each with a single joint in the middle, forming a knee. The foot was triangular, with the base of the triangle forward. A tubular flexible toe grew from each point of the triangle. The point at the heel had its own toe.

The next segment upward was about the same, growing arms with single joints forming elbows. The triangular hands were somewhat smaller than the feet and the fingers were longer and thinner than the toes.

The next segment was the same, except that the arms ended in thick claws instead of the triangular hands.

The top segment was the head. There were two upright slits on the forehead section, two clear rounded bumps below the slits that Z assumed were eyes, two narrow horizontal slits below the eyes and an upright slit for a mouth that worked from side to side, instead of up and down. The thing was a clear pale golden-tan coloration all over and was covered in plastic-like material. It was carrying some kind of wand. It had two short antennae that waved around constantly.

"That can't be a robot! It wouldn't work worth a damn!" he exclaimed to Ape, as it moved into the room. It ignored him and went to the ring to which Joe's rope was attached. It did something to the ring, which lifted to reveal an opening behind. There was a plastic bowl in the panel it took out to hand to Joe. The small bowl contained a yellow paste.

It closed the panel, then went to Thing's ring, where it repeated the process. When it went on to ET's ring, Z watched carefully. It seemed to pull the ring outward, lift and twist the ring to the right in one motion. The panel opened and it handed the bowl to ET and closed the panel.

The thing went toward Bear very cautiously. Bear watched it carefully – so Bear was known by that thing to be dangerous. File that!

It opened the panel and handed the bowl to Bear, who made no move toward it.

The thing approached Z, paused and went on toward Ape. Ape unsheathed long claws and took a swipe at it, but it jumped back and wasn't hit. It stared at Ape a few moments, then came toward Z. Z waited until it was at the ring and dived at it, but his hands slid off the hard, smooth chitin. The thing jumped back and stared at Z a moment before going out of the room. The door closed and Z looked at Ape.

"Well! I guess we don't get any grub," he said with a grin. Ape grinned back. Z had never seen such a mouthful of sharp teeth.

Z went to the ring and inspected it. He also inspected the wall behind it, but could detect no seams.

He grasped the ring, lifted, pulled and twisted clockwise. The panel opened. There was a bowl of the yellow paste inside, which he put a bit of on his tongue.

"Hmmm. Not bad. Probably nutritious as all hell."

He inspected the bowl, but it was a soft, tough plastic that wouldn't tear or break.

"No sharp edges," he grumbled. He ate a bit of the stuff and placed the bowl back inside the panel, then dropped the lid and twisted the ring back upright. The panel was motored shut "Like the trunk lid on a Cadillac."

He heard a sharp thumping behind him and turned to see Ape hitting the wall. When Z looked at him, Ape pointed to his ring and put a palm upward.

"Oh. OK," Z said. "Watch closely."

He repeated opening his panel, using greatly exaggerated

motions, and watched as Ape copied him, opening his own panel. Ape ate most of the glop in his bowl, then shrugged at Z, who indicated he should put the bowl back into the panel and close the lid.

He was in the process of sitting back on the floor when his eye caught Ape's panel motoring shut. He jumped back to his feet to stare at the panel – and to get the glimmer of an idea.

"Ape, old boy, I've got it!" he cried excitedly. "When that worm thing comes back in here, one of these times, it'll get the shock of its life!"

Z again sat to consider his – their situation. The floor was a comfortably warm temperature, as was the wall. The air was good and was very pleasantly clean-smelling. There was no way to tell where the light was coming from. This could be a specially made room smack-dab in downtown Sarasota, but something was telling him that wasn't nearly the case. Something made him think he was a very long way from Florida!

He was lighter! That was it! When he moved, his actions were just a bit too much. He was compensating for weight that wasn't there – there being Earth; ergo, he was in a spaceship!

Just great! He always had been smart. If he had actually been picked up by some kind of alien spaceship, he had some explaining to do – to himself. After all, hadn't he been the one to always say that kind of stuff was really a silly bunch of crap?

Z shook his head and saw Ape watching him. He said, "I want my mommie!" and grinned. He got one of Ape's toothy grins, in return.

OK. The door opened upward, took about ten seconds after the click and buzz and ... and.... There was a featureless white wall eight or ten feet away from the opening opposite. That wasn't really a whole lot to know. Maybe some of it could be used, someday, but that didn't help much, right now. He sensed the vibration had now stopped and put a palm against the wall. Nothing. He was amused when Ape did the same thing, then looked puzzled at him.

"We're in orbit – or whatever," he explained. "They've shut down the drive engines. Maybe we're in free fall. It must take a hell of a long time to come...!"

Oh, cripes almighty! All the creatures in this room came from different worlds! He was just the latest acquisition! That meant faster-than-light travel was possible!

He'd been right about one thing. Now, he'd like to go home, please, so he could say "Nyah! Nyah! Nyah!" in their faces.

Was that what that creepy feeling was, just before he'd decided the main engines had shut down? That thing like a sort of sudden vertigo in his mind?

Well, at least, he wouldn't have his name on front of any of those supermarket tabloids saying his kid was an alien!

He giggled to himself. He hoped they didn't have any way to knock up a male from Earth!

Think! He had to think! All this muddle wasn't getting him anywhere. If there's a way in, there's a way out.

Oh, yes? Really? And what if "out" is lightyears away? Dr. Who, where are you when I need you?

Z stood and looked around the room at his five fellow captives. They had all taken some interest in him – except Bear, who was now sitting, facing the wall. He apparently didn't care for any of their company.

Come on! Be fair! The guy was as scared as any of them. He'd been kidnaped by aliens, too.

Z reopened the food panel to inspect the smooth edges very carefully. They seemed to be of perfect sharpness, which was why, when closed, they showed no seam.

He ran a finger along the lower edge, discovering it cut like a razor. He pulled the rope along the edge and it cut, but not through. The edge was much too short a line to sever the rope completely. If he had about three times that length of edge, it wouldn't be any problem, whatever. That the rope cut at all showed its strength was against tearing. It didn't have much resistance to shear.

Good! He'd hoped for that!

He turned the rope over to try to cut it from the other side and watched it "grow" together where he'd just cut, leaving no evidence it had ever been tampered with. He tried it and it was as strong as before. Cutting and having it grow back didn't weaken anything.

He looked into the panel and upward at the hidden hinges. They were enclosed and unreachable. He couldn't drop a pin or something to get the lid off.

He wanted something for a weapon, not to cut the rope. He knew how to do that, but just being free of the rope wasn't being free. It simply would allow a bit of extra movement.

Ape was watching all this and would try each process after Z. He yanked on the rope and pulled with all his might, which was considerable, then shrugged at Z.

Z grinned and said, "If you can't break it, a bulldozer can't break it!" Even the nylon and polypropylene ropes he was familiar with would have a weight test of more than a ton for a rope that thick. There was no reason to doubt for one minute this was much stronger per unit gage.

Z studied the panel carefully, grinned, took a deep breath, placed the rope across the lower part of the opening, and pulled the lid down onto it. He pressed down hard and twisted the ring upright, making a silent prayer the motor was as strong as he hoped.

It was! The motor pulled the panel shut, neatly severing a piece of the rope inside. Z was reopening his panel when he saw Ape preparing to cut his rope the same way. He must not!

"Ape! No! Don't cut the rope!" he cried.

Ape turned toward him and cocked his head to the side. Z signaled for him not to cut the rope. Ape stared for a moment, then dropped the rope. He shrugged.

"I wish I could make you understand, Ape," he said, hoping the tone of his voice would deliver the message English words couldn't. "We have to wait to see if there's some kind of alarm if a rope's cut. If a guard comes, you'll still know how to cut it – and you'll also know how much time you'll have to act, once you do. If no one comes, we'll know they have no alarm."

Ape wouldn't understand him, of course. He wished the big fellow could. He wished a lot of things.

He turned back to the panel to finish opening it. He took out the short severed rope section and pressed one end to the piece hanging from the ring. It "grew" together.

He laughed. So far, it was going just like he hoped. Make the plan as you go along. Test each stage of the game and be absolutely certain you don't miss anything. Be thorough – all things against his nature, but he knew he was capable of disciplining himself when the occasion required. There wouldn't be any second chances here, and it was altogether too possible there were no chances at all. Even if he could get the upper hand, somehow, there was no way he could force them to take him back home.

Something else against his nature was letting anyone get away with doing things like this to him!

Cross that bridge when you come to it.

Cliché time! Oh, well!

Z stared a moment at the severed end of his rope, then said, "I'm going to move around the room a bit to see if they have some sort of bug in here that'll tell them I've gotten loose. If they don't know I cut the rope – we don't know that yet, by the way – the test isn't over until it's over. Maybe they won't have anything that'll tell them if

I'm moving around where I shouldn't be, either, see?

"Why am I saying all this? No one here understands me. I have to talk or go mad, guys."

He slowly moved to the center of the room, where he walked around for a couple of minutes, but nothing else happened.

"I guess they can't see me or don't even care. There's not one single damned thing I can do to them, locked in this room – except to make plans. I can always make a few plans. If they don't work, I'm the only one in the world – I mean in the whole damned universe – who'll know!"

He went to where little Joe was huddled in the corner. As he approached, the little animal hugged tighter against the wall. It tore at Z's heart. He knelt and held out a hand. Joe stared at it, but didn't move.

"Come on, little guy. Let's make friends," he said softly.

Joe slowly reached out to touch his hand, then began trembling violently and made gasping sounds. Z pulled Joe to him and held the terrified little animal against himself.

"Poor little fellow. You're scared out of your mind! Damn!

"We all are, little guy. We all are.

"You don't know where you are, you don't know what any of us are, you don't know why and you don't understand any of it.

"That's the worst part. None of us understands what's going on."

The trembling of the animal was lessening.

"I always was a sucker for any defenseless animal in trouble. I love animals. Anytime I ever saw an animal mistreated, I'd want to kill the stupid bastard that did it. Kick at a dog, whip a horse, starve a cat – it doesn't matter. I can't stand that sort of thing.

"I'll get us out of this, little guy. I promise."

The creature clung to him, and didn't want to let go. He gently dislodged it and sat it back against the wall, then went to ET. ET held out a hand to him before he got there.

"I guess that means I've already got your support," he said. The creature looked steadily and directly into his eyes. It tightened its grip, then let go.

Well, Joe couldn't do much. He was too afraid and didn't seem to have a lot of intelligence. Obviously, ET would actively and intelligently help. Ape's help was foregone. There was already rapport between them.

He hoped.

He approached Bear, but was warned off with a growl.

"Have it your way, Pal. I think you should try to make friends instead of running them off. You may need them."

He saw the tentacled being watching him. He went over and looked at it.

"You're really kind of spooky. I mean, you talk about an alien! I really meant what I said to Bear about us being friends and I ... hey!"

The little creature ran up his leg and quickly wrapped the two lower tentacles around his waist to put one of the upper tentacles around his neck and the other against the side of his face.

"Cripes! You scared hell out of me!

"You know, you don't feel so bad at all. I was worried you'd be slimy, or something. You're kind of warm and rubbery – like that blue silicone goo they use for gaskets. For some reason, you're sort of, I don't know, relaxing.

"Let go now. I have to see everyone."

He disentangled himself from Thing and put it back on the floor. It couldn't be of any real help. It was just some dumb animal, probably from a water world of some kind or other. It didn't have any intelligence.

As he approached Ape, Ape put out a hand. He was grasped in a kind of Roman handshake as Ape reached over and took the other hand. It formed a double Roman handshake, with their wrists making the center of an X. Ape grinned the toothy grin, and he returned it.

"You know, big guy, I'm glad you're a friendly sort! If you weren't, I'd be small pieces about now!"

They heard the click from the door and Z dived to his rope. He pressed the ends together, watching as they "grew" into one piece. There was no evidence it had ever been off the tether. If they knew he could move about at will, things might get very hairy for him.

He turned to see six of the "worm" things entering through the open doorway. These were slightly darker than the feeder and were carrying some sort of wands. The wands were about eighteen inches long and were affixed on a triangular base about five inches across. The wide part of the base was against the palm of the hand and the short wand extended off the point. The base contained three buttons, one orange, one green and one black. The base rested so it was easy for them to reach the buttons. There was a line from the base to a box that seemed glued to the head. There were no straps or such to hold the boxes in place. They just rested atop the creature.

Each of the "worms" went to one of the tethered group and touched the wand to the rope where it passed through the ring. The rope fell away.

File that. The wands serve a lot of purposes on this ship, it seems. The earlier "worm" had used it to open the door as it went out and to close it as it came in. It was also used to release the ropes, possibly with some kind of coded electrical signal. Probably frequency-controlled.

Ape slashed at his guard, and was touched with the wand. He was thrown hard against the wall and to the floor, where he lay a moment, moaning. Z rushed at the guard, yelling, "You crummy bastard! I'll...!"

He was touched by the wand his guard held. It as like

being hit with a very large, very heavy, very hot steel ball. He was flung off his feet to lay gasping on the metal floor until the feeling he was in a pot of boiling water subsided, a few long seconds that seemed like hours.

"You sleazy bastards! You're dead meat! All of you! I swear that before God! I'm going to personally kill every one of you scum. Count on it. You're a bunch of dead mothers!"

That was another use of the wands. Weapons. Z was going to need a weapon. Oh, yes! He was going to need something that would knock these – *things* around a bit!

The others were being led out the door as he got back to his feet. Ape turned to grin at him and to make a strange sign with his fingers. The sign may be new to Z, but the meaning was unmistakable.

He returned the grin and made "the middle finger" sign at his guard. His guard pulled on the rope and he followed it out into a curved hallway, where Z noticed the guard had wrapped the rope around its upper arm.

That wasn't very smart!

He moved up toward the guard, then suddenly stopped, set his feet and yanked the rope back as hard as he could. The guard was slammed against the wall, but spun out and jabbed at him with the wand. He held up his hands and stood still. The guard turned and pulled the rope.

"Just so you know, Plastic Head!"

He remembered the reaction of the feeder, or lack of it, when he and Ape had tried to harm it. "You bastards don't feel any emotions at all, do you?" He sneered at the guard's back as they went along the hallway.

They were moving slowly, the guard shuffling along instead of taking normal steps.

Why would they design such smooth floors in their ships, when they weren't designed to move on polished surfaces?

Z began to think the true bosses, his real captors, were probably very different from these things. These were probably not intelligent, themselves, but were trained to handle the prisoners, like German Shepherds were trained to handle sheep.

Well, Steven P. Zutec was *not* a sheep!

He noticed differing patterns on the various door panels as they passed by them. He wasn't sure whether the signs represented numbers or were indications of what was inside the room. Too bad they weren't pictures! He could find one that looked like – like what? What would the equivalent of a gun look like, here? He would have to try to learn something about what the things meant. Why a triangle?

He was stopped in front of a door with a black square on it, which the guard tapped with the end of the wand. The door slid silently upward after about ten seconds. The guard pointed inside with the wand and Z entered.

File that. Hit the center of the symbol with the wand to open the door.

There were various sizes and shapes of low benches around a complicated console by the left wall as they entered. The guard pointed at the console with the wand.

Z stood still. Time to see how far he could push.

"What the hell do you want, Turdhead?"

The guard pointed at the benches.

Better not take it too far with the trained dog. He'd end up with a trained "bite!" response.

Z chose a comfortable-looking bench and sat. He studied all he could see carefully, but none of it made any sense to him. He noted there was an oversized TV-type screen that was, apparently, three dimensional or something, because it was as thick as it was high and long. There were hundreds of assorted sockets and connections on panel boards on the console and around in other places.

Some sort of control room?

Then, why bring him here?

The guard went to the rear of the room and tapped the wall. A door slid open and another of the "worms" came into the room. It was carrying a complicated helmet that trailed two cords. One cord had a microphone on the end and the other had a very complicated plug. This one was an amber color, but was, otherwise, exactly the same as the guard. This wasn't one of the captors, then?

The guard held the wand close to Z while the other placed the helmet on his head. He sat very still.

Was this some kind of brainwashing device?

That didn't make any sense!

The plug from the helmet was placed into a shaped socket on the console. Suddenly the guard started jabbing at Z with the wand, not touching him, but coming very close.

"Hey! What the hell did I do? If you touch me with that thing again, I'll take you apart, right here, you miserable asshole!"

The new "worm" picked up the microphone. It spoke into it and Z heard a hollow-sounding voice in his head: "It will not touch you unless you make it necessary. It was necessary to get a strong neural path plotting to analyze and match your basic speech response to what the machine has."

It waved for the guard to move away, then adjusted several switches and dials on the console.

"Just be quiet and we will perform some tests. There will be no unnecessary pain – if you cooperate."

"I'll be dog-damned! A real translator/computer, and you didn't have to program my language in! Wow!"

The voice in his head instructed, "It is not necessary that you vocalize random thoughts. That tends to slur your mind patterns and run them together. Concentrate and hold to one thought clearly. You will soon learn to use the machine."

It made a few more adjustments.

"You will not speak, except to answer questions that I have posed. I am your tester. I wish to determine if your species is of any use."

"You damned arrogant *bug*!" Z thought. The globe whined over his head.

"Your thoughts do not translate. It is necessary that the terms of your thoughts translate clearly into my language. The tone of your thoughts is unpleasant. Suppress them, or you will suffer the consequences," the voice threatened.

"You disgusting worm! I'm supposed to let a thing like you mess around in my mind?

"Well, Puke Puss, let's get something straight right now! I'm not about to... OW!"

The guard had lightly brushed his arm with the wand.

"Hey! I can't help it if I think you're purely scuzz!" Z yelled.

"Possibly, but it is unnecessary to transmit the thought. Lower the volume of your response."

"How do I not transmit my thoughts?" Z demanded.

"Do not think," the "worm" replied.

"Oh, don't be a ridiculous ass!" Z cried. "You can't just stop *thinking*!"

There was a pause while the "worm" studied him. "Yes, I can. Do you tell me you cannot?"

"Yes, damnit! I can't just turn it off!"

"How very odd," the voice said, after another pause. "What is your functional position?"

"What the hell is a functional position?" Z snapped.

"Your answer is muddled with irrelevant interjections. What are your duties in the hive – or your society?"

"I don't understand," Z replied.

The "worm" now began to fidget a bit. "What is your

societally designated caste position? What is your ... functional area?"

"You still don't make any sense," Z answered. "If you mean, what was my job, I'm a computer programmer, part of the time, and a pilot of small planes, other times. I'm a damned good small engine mechanic, like outboards and lawn mowers and that kind of thing, and I can pretty well handle any kind of business machinery, like copiers. I can play a wicked guitar and...."

"Wait! Stop!" The voice was so strong it hurt. "Are you then a multifunctional, even outside of your ... area?"

"Of course I'm multifunctional! Isn't everybody?"

Z felt he had a solid lever here if he could figure how to use it. Maybe he could confuse the tester so it would give up questioning him. These things were bugs, so thought like bugs! Most bugs didn't do a lot of things. They did just one. They just ate leaves or dug holes or something. The captors made the mistake of having some damned bug ask questions of someone who didn't think like a bug!

Another thing to file. If you just let your thoughts roam and don't concentrate on anything, the translator doesn't react.

The voice was back. "You will now remove the headgear and return to your cell with the guard. I am not educated to work with such an undisciplined mind. I will find a proper tester."

"Wait!" Z cried. "I don't know what's happening here! Who and what are you? What do you want from me?"

"I am a tester. I learn positions. I am a third caste high. If I were to speak my personal designation, it would translate as 'worm' to you.

"What you heard was supplied by your own mind. If you wish to hear my singular denotation, you may lift the headgear."

Z lifted the helmet and the "worm" said, "Zeekou."

"Zee Koo," Z repeated. "Zeekou." He pointed to himself and said, "I'm called Z."

Zeekou's mouth flew open – to the sides. It didn't work up and down. It pointed to the helmet in Z's hands. Z put it on.

"What?"

"Your personal designation is Z?"

"Yeah. Why?"

"My own is Zeekou. The first part, Zee, denotes that I am the highest position in my caste. I have two syllables, which denotes third caste. 'Kou' says I am a tester. In my society, if you have one syllable you are the top caste. Zee, your denotation, would mean highest position. A second caste high has very specialized talents. The only higher is a no-syllable. There are very few.

"You may then understand why I was taken aback by your own personal denotation. I had not considered the qualifications emplaced by a different societal structure of the differing customs as to positional references."

"I see," Z said. "Would you tell me something?"

"What is that?"

"You communicate with sound, but I don't see any ears. Where are they?"

Zeekou pointed at the upper slits and antennae. "Go with the guard, now. I will find a qualified tester."

Z went with the guard, paying very special attention to the symbols on the doors. They didn't mean any more this time. They must just be markers. "Go to square and bring me a brickbat. I'll be in circle," or something.

The guard entered the room they were being held in, again tapping the center of the symbol with the wand. It took him to the same ring and attached the rope by passing it through the ring and touching it to itself around the ring, then it left.

Joe and ET were at their rings. Ape was brought in after

a few minutes. Joe was very agitated and held out a hand to Z. Z began singing what he could remember of "Blowin' In the Wind" very softly.

It seemed to help.

Z sat against the wall to think. He could confuse these bugs, but what would he do if he met his captors? Could he hope to confuse them, even slightly?

The first thing to do would be to get one of those wands. A weapon would make all the difference.

He was alone, here, for the moment. He had no idea what the fate of the others might be, but if all they were doing was testing, they would be back – unless they failed the test?

What was the test all about?

He had been asked what his job had been.

Was he to be a slave? A skilled slave?

Surely, a society that had space travel wouldn't ever use slaves!

They did kidnap, though.

It was all so very confusing. If he kept on thinking about this sort of thing, there was no hope he would find a plan. He must discipline his actions, but his mind was, to this point, refusing to cooperate. That had to change. He *must* force himself to remain fixed on one path.

About twenty minutes later the door opened and Thing was dragged in. It spotted Z and tried to reach him, but the guard yanked the rope, sending it sliding into the wall.

"Hey, asshole!" Z yelled. "If you mistreat that animal one more time, I'll break you in half!"

The guard turned to stare at Z.

Z pointed to himself and said, "Z."

The guard stared.

Z picked up his rope and pointed to Thing, waved his rope and pointed to his attachment ring, then to Thing again.

The guard hesitated, then slowly brought Thing over. Z

took the rope from the guard and ran it through his ring, where he pressed the end against the rope and it "grew" together. The guard stepped back to consider, then turned and left the room.

Thing ran up Z's leg and put its tentacles around his waist and neck and against the side of his face. Z stroked the little animal and looked over to Ape, who grinned his toothy grin.

Ape was still attached to his ring. He waited for the guard to leave, then banged the wall for Z's attention. Z put a palm upward.

Ape held up his rope and pointed to his panel and held a palm upward. Z shook his head "no," then sat on the floor. Thing seemed content to sit in his lap with the tentacle against the side of his face. The strange little animal seemed to have a relaxing effect on him for some reason, and he was able to think more clearly and to keep his mind on one subject. Still, he wasn't forming any viable plan. His mind began to drift to strange subjects and wonders.

This hadn't caught up to him yet. He wasn't at all sure he wouldn't go into some kind of panic reaction at any moment. His mind was almost chaotic.

He sighed and leaned back against the warm wall to stare around the room. A few minutes later, the feeder came in to pick up the bowls spotted around. It went to the row of lights to Z's left and touched one of them, a panel slid open, it threw the bowls in, touched another light, and the panel slid closed.

File that! Touch the lights to open and close the garbage bin! It was surely big enough to hide in – unless it was an automatic incinerator or something such. That would have to be looked into, but was something to bear in mind.

Z didn't take his eyes off the bug.

It turned to go and made the mistake of walking too close to Ape, who lifted a leg and kicked it a tremendous blow on the posterior of the lower segment, sending it sliding across the room and into the far wall. Z thoroughly expected to see Ape punished with the wand, but the feeder just got up and left the room. It simply didn't react. It didn't become angered or seek any kind of revenge.

File that, too! Figure out what these bugs are!

Z turned to Ape and said, "Too bad Bear wasn't there. You two could've played ping-pong with that thing!"

Ape put a palm upward and shrugged. The big hairy fellow was as puzzled as Z by the lack of retaliation.

"We can't think like bugs," he said to Ape. "Maybe they don't even feel pain, so they have no response for what we find to be a painful situation. That gives us an edge.

"I wish you could understand me. It would help if we all knew what was going on in the same way."

The best part of an hour passed before another guard came in. It came directly to Z to release his rope, while taking absolutely no notice of the fact Thing was still attached to Z's ring.

Z disentangled himself from Thing, put the little animal on the floor and patted it. He followed the guard to the same room he was in before with Zeekou. The helmet was still on the bench where he had left it, so he put it on and sat to wait with the guard standing motionless beside him.

The guard-bug as much as expected him to put on the helmet. Remember that bit. These lesser slaves weren't capable of feeling even mild surprise – *but* Zeekou had definitely registered strong surprise. Were these guards so different? Why? How?

After a few minutes wait, the door in the rear opened and another "worm" entered. Z noticed this one was darker than Zeekou, who was darker than the guards, who were darker than the feeder. Something added up about the bugs!

The "worm" picked up the microphone and said, "If you

will lift the helmet I will give my personal designation."

Z lifted the helmet and heard a sound like "Eerf." He then replaced the helmet and said. "Eerf. One syllable. I figured you were some sort of bigshot when I saw you were darker than Zeekou."

He watched the reaction of this one, who also seemed to register surprise. He had been right! Now to go further, when the chance came. Keep it off balance.

"You were able to so deduce I am of higher caste than is Zeekou because I am of darker hue? You deduce this from only two examples?

"Amazing! Perhaps you will have some use, after all!"

Z sneered. "I have four examples. The feeder is very pale, almost white. The guards are only slightly darker. Zeekou is quite a bit darker than the guards and has explained he has more status. You come in and you are darker than Zeekou. I, therefore, thoroughly expected you to have a one syllable name and to be higher than Zeekou. It is only simple logic."

He watched Eerf's reactions closely, which were a pause to think, then a slow reply, carefully considered.

"You do not know how rare it is the ability to solve such problems with limited data," Eerf replied (Yeah! Among *bugs*! Z thought, but was able to keep that from the helmet). "You have a high intelligence.

"However, I am thus programmed to understand these random-factor intelligences. On some rare occasions, they have proven useful. They can solve specific problems, even when there is no basis in logic. They can create their own fields of inquiry. We must sometimes seek out such a mind."

Now Z was puzzled. Was this bug trying to surprise or shock him?

"Eerf, you seem to find high intelligence to be a negative thing. Why?"

Eerf paused to consider each time before it spoke.

"Intelligence of a random type is anti-survival. Races that develop it tend to be great discoverers and creators until the time they eventually learn the basics of matter physics, then use the information in attempts to subjugate their own species. The result is then both obvious and inevitable, but they ignore that. They always seem to thus destroy themselves. Only two great civilizations in the known history of this part of the local galaxy, so far as we know, have survived past their initial attempts to reach other star systems."

Z stared directly into Eerf's eyes. This was it! This was what he wanted to say. He had to get a strong reaction from this one! It would tell him whether these bugs could be truly shocked – or not!

"They built this ship?" he asked, offhandedly.

"Amazing!" Eerf shouted sharply, hurting Z's head in the helmet. "You have deduced that you are on a ship! Your deduction they built this ship is erroneous, however. We built the ship."

Oh, no! Not even maybe! There was only one possible explanation for that statement, if it was even partly true.

Z sneered. "But you did *not* invent it! You've admitted you're uncreative, so there's simply no way you invented the ships!"

The pause was a little longer this time. It almost seemed this bug was getting instructions. A radio in the ear slits?

"Yes," Eerf admitted. "They had invented the ships and the machinery and we learned thus to copy the work."

"So you just take what others develop and steal if for uses of your own. You're really big deals, aren't you?"

Eerf waved a hand and said, "Your thoughts do not translate well. Your thoughts are muddled. Try to control them.

"What is your official caste position in the culture from

which you were taken?"

It came back to that!

"I told Zeekou I do many things. I can't help it if you're too limited to understand that."

"We do not require your assistance in those areas," Eerf replied seriously.

"What the hell are you talking about?!" Z exploded. "You take off on some weird tangent and I don't know what you're talking about!"

"You stated you are not able to give us assistance on problems of limitations," Eerf answered.

"'Help it?'" Z laughed. "That's an idiom, you idiot!"

Eerf was beginning to become agitated. He said, "Please do not use idioms. They are without context and tend to muddle translations, too. You must control your thoughts. I find you thence confusing."

"Oh, you do?" thought Z, directing it to the helmet. "Well, if you're confused by idioms, just think how confused you'll be when my mind goes into overdrive!"

Eerf was amazed by his ability to deduce the obvious, so keep it off balance with the idioms and random thoughts.

"What is this overdrive?" Eerf asked, shakily.

Either this would work or he would pay a high price, but it was too late to turn back now! Go for it!

"Overdrive is an involuntary state the human mind may reach when it's necessary to find a solution to a difficult problem. We can't control it well, so don't use such as the translator machines. It confuses machines, though I don't know why. It's really very logical, to me.

"The trouble is, whenever I think of overdrive in a tense situation, I sometimes shift into that phase. As a matter of fact I'm shifting right now!

"Sorry, Turdhead, but you asked for it!

"So you see, the gastrointestinal fortuitous tetracycline upwardly mobile cycle is pre-empting the formaldehyde type preservative mulch reaction of the reactionary reflexes of Super Glue, or super manhood, or womanhood, isn't relevant to an elephant or any other pachyderm because of amelioration of the transcendental gizmos and gained transductional morphisms, if you see what I mean."

"Control now your thoughts!" Eerf yelled. It was actually dancing around in agitation.

"It's generally part of the ultra-interdemonstrable – intra? – functional suppressed mode usology of certain gaspingly filial totalitarian conceptual references.

"Right?" Z sighed, in relief. He hadn't been punished with the wand and Eerf was demolished. The bug was like a worm on a hot rock.

"Remove the headset! Take it off!" Eerf shouted.

Just before he removed the helmet Z thought, "A wop mama lubah ba lop bam boom!"

He handed the helmet to Eerf. "Tuitti fruitti, bug!" he added aloud.

The guard took him back to his cell. He was reattached to the ring-pin and Thing immediately ran up his leg to its now-accustomed position with the tentacle against his face.

He immediately felt good! He was learning fast! They would be forced to take him directly to the real authority here!

ET was asleep, as was Joe, who was rolled into a fetal ball. Bear wasn't there. Ape looked a question at him.

"I can't answer, Ape. No words. Sorry."

As he spoke Thing stroked the side of his face with the tentacle tip.

"So that's it. You hear with the tentacle, do you?"

He stood, reaching to his ring, and opened the panel. Ape was watching him attentively. He put his palm out and shook his head. Ape sat and watched.

He took the bowl, which had been refilled, and ate some

of the gruel. He offered some to Thing, who touched it with the tentacle, touched the glop on the tentacle tip to its mouth and drew back.

"Oh-ho! So you taste a difference, do you?

"Very useful knowledge. We all get different foods. Mine's different than yours, so we'll have to get you back over there for your meals.

"Wait, for now, though."

He put the empty bowl back and closed the panel, then sat and dozed.

He suddenly jerked wide awake. He was momentarily confused, but the door was opening. The click had awakened him. A guard was entering. It came directly to him to release his rope. He held Thing's rope against the wand tip and it fell open, too. He ignored the guard as he took Thing to its own ring and attached the rope. He then opened the panel and handed Thing the bowl. He wanted to observe the effect of this. He wanted to make the guard react.

As he closed the panel, he muttered, "Think that one over, Plastic Head!"

Nothing whatever. The guard simply stood there until he was through.

He turned to wave for the guard to lead on. It took him to the next room down the curved hall from where he had been taken before. The room had benches like the first one, but the console was many times more complicated than the other had been. He sat on a bench and waited.

He soon heard someone – or something – approaching from behind, but made up his mind he wouldn't turn around.

A soft, feminine voice said, "Good evening."

He forgot his resolve and spun toward the voice. There was a human woman standing there. Almost.

She was more humanoid than any of the others, but was thick around the waist and had huge mammaries. Her lips were wide and thick and her eyes showed no white. She had long, coarse, blond hair and skin a shade lighter than Z. When she spoke, the voice came from a speaker over the console.

"The machine has analyzed your speech and will hereafter automatically translate for the both of us. I am trained in the history of intelligence and feel I can find a basis to use in communication, even with such as you."

Z took an immediate strong dislike to her. He resented her arrogance and her condescending manner.

"I am, as I said, a historian. We may be able to talk, quite easily. My name is Pressa Doe Geep. My society uses more syllables to denote rank than do the Pweetoos, who use less.

"I understand you are denoted Z, a single syllable. In my society, you are of the lowest rank with your one syllable."

That does it! thought Z. "You fail to understand," he said, in a syrupy voice. "Z isn't my name, it's only my nickname. My full name is Stev-en Par-ker 'Zoot' Zu-tec.

"As you can see, it is far too many syllables for people to use every time they wish to address me. The 'Zoot' is the base name. It is in special marks that denote it's my nickname base. It starts with Z.

"My culture has what we call an alphabetically linear structured connotation. The alphabet consists of twenty six denoting letters, starting with A and ending with Z. This gives us twenty six ranks. The closer to A and farther from Z, the lower the rank.

"I am a Z, the highest rank. The Zoot, or denoting base name, is next to the last, or sirename.

"In my own case, I have a Z denotation before my *two* syllable last name. You would have a D denotation next to your *one* syllable sirename.

"I'll call you Doe, from your denoting position next to the sirename. It's unfortunate that it's only D. D is, let's see, A B C D. Only four removed from the lowest rank.

"I hope that's clear, Doe?"

He gazed calmly at her, in total innocence. This was a silly exchange, in his opinion, meant only to gain some odd psychological advantage. He may as well use it to see if he could gain an advantage from her reaction, but he was disappointed. She was obviously no higher in the hierarchy than the bugs.

Them's the nasty breaks of life! She was now clearly upset.

"You can see your arrogance is misplaced," he added.

"Very well," she said. "Names are of no real importance here."

"I'm glad that's settled," he replied.

"Yes. Well, perhaps, if I understood some of your race's history, I could find a satisfactory basis for communicating the Pweetoos' needs to you," she continued.

Z smiled at her, thought a moment and said, "Why not, I ask you a question and you ask me one. The would seem fair to both of us."

She waved a hand. "No, no! It is not necessary that I give you information. It is you who are being tested."

"Then you can forget it! I'm not answering any of your questions!"

"If I call the guard, you *will* answer!" she threatened.

"Hell! Call it! I may be forced to answer questions, but you won't know if I'm lying!"

"This is most distressing!" she cried. "Why will you not cooperate?"

"Oh, I'll be more than happy to cooperate," Z snapped. "To cooperate means a giving and taking, not just a giving. What you propose is that I willingly submit to one-way interrogation by you. That, I refuse!"

She wrung her hands. Z sensed a subterfuge that he couldn't quite place. "Why would you wish to know about me?" she asked. "I simply work in the employ of the Pweetoos."

"You misunderstand," Z replied. "I couldn't care less about you. I want to know about these – what did you call them? – Pweetoos?"

She stared at the floor.

"How could such a race take over the galaxy?" he asked.

"Oh, no, no, no! They don't control the galaxy!" she retorted. "They control but a very small area in this galactic sector. A few thousand star systems."

"Only a few thousand star systems? I never dreamed they were such small potatoes!"

"They are not vegetables," she replied.

"What? I meant...." Z stammered. "Look. Small potatoes is just an idiom, an expression. It only means they're not very important to anything."

She still looked confused. "Please do not use idiom clauses," she begged.

She checked her notes. "What was your function in your society before the Pweetoos took you?"

He thought a moment. "I guess it would be simplest to say I was a programmer of business computers. I made programs and built mathematical forms. In addition, I pilot small aircraft from place to place around the planet, carrying passengers and cargo. I did some other things, at times." He stopped to see her reaction. "I trust that's clear, so far?"

"Yes," she answered. "I was told that you functioned on several levels. I can see that programming of a business computer is basically the same as the programming of flight computers. There is no real diversity."

"The aircraft is flown manually," Z stated.

"It is not computer directed?' she asked.

"It is flown manually."

"I was told by ... you are multifunctional. Perhaps it is true, or perhaps there is a language deficiency. We must be certain," she said and turned to speak into a microphone on the console. The speaker made a whining and clicking noise and the guard left the room.

"There is a possible problem with translation. I have sent for a remedy."

"There's nothing wrong with the language," Z retorted. "I program computers, fly airplanes, repair small engines – no, don't say it. The engines run on fossil fuels – have been a physical laborer on fishing boats and have worked construction, light and heavy, and am *very* good with electronic equipment.

"So there!"

She stared hard at him. Why did he get the feeling she was being ... devious?

"I can do almost anything I set my mind to do. I'm not so limited as your precious Pweetoos," he spat at her.

She fidgeted (a little too rehearsed?). "It is my turn to ask a question."

"You just did," he replied. "I answered it. It's my turn.

"How did the Pweetoos get control of these ships, and why do the owners allow them to use their technology for such silly purposes as this?"

She was (acting?) confused. "Z, the Pweetoos were discovered on their original planet by the original Maitan people. The Maitans were exploring much of the galactic arm, back then, and would allow certain of the cultures they found to join them in their explorations to gather knowledge.

"The Pweetoos were allowed to join them and were able to breed individuals who were superbly fitted for piloting the ships.

"Over the course of time, the Pweetoos added to the

crews of the ships until there were far too many to be resisted, so they took over the ships.

"The Maitans had a language, both written and spoken, that was more versatile than any found before or since, so it is used generally, today.

"The Pweetoos can copy almost anything. They copy very exactly, which is why all markings on the ships are in the Old Maitan. The markings were on the original, thus are on the copies.

"When the Pweetoos then felt they had learned all that the Maitans could teach them, they eliminated them, before they became a danger to the Pweetoo culture."

"Wait a goddamned minute!" Z shouted. "You said those bugs 'eliminated' the Maitans. What did you mean?"

Doe looked confused again (Z felt she was acting and had that one down pat!). "They eliminated them."

Z was aghast. "You mean killed them?"

"That is what it means to eliminate a living thing," she replied, without emotion.

"You mean they killed off an entire race?"

"Of course. They were of no further use." She seemed unable to understand his reaction. (*Seemed.* What was so phony about her?)

"That's the most coldblooded...! I can...! What the hell is going on here?!" he exploded, unbelieving. "How can you be so totally..!?" (She almost smirked. What was she doing? Why?)

The guard came in, carrying a very complicated helmet with a great many wires trailing behind. The wires ended in several complicated sockets. It handed the device to Doe and left. Doe pulled leads from the console and plugged them into the lines from the helmet.

"That is why we use this method of teaching," she said, as though nothing had happened. "The headgear will teach you to read and write Maitan and you will be able to speak it very exactly. I have already said it is the most versatile language ever discovered. We can then converse without these restrictions of insufficient language translations from the machines."

She set some controls on the console. "Please place the headgear."

"Wait!" Z pleaded as he placed the helmet. "Does this mean that, if I fail the tests, I'll be eliminated?"

"If you are of no use." (Studied innocence?)

He gaped at her.

"But ... Bear!" he cried. "Bear didn't come back! Did these *things* eliminate Bear?"

"What is this Bear?"

"The black and white furry being who was being held in the cell with us."

"Yes. It was too aggressive and uncooperative. It defied the Pweetoos. They will not be defied."

He was still gaping at her.

"A mistake when selecting it. It proved totally unsuitable," she continued. "It was a professional fighter in an arena for the amusement of spectators. It was, therefore, unsuitable as a testee."

Z yelled, "You mean you take some gladiator, who fights for his living, and kill him, because he fights?!"

"Of course. He was useless. Please lower your voice."

"And I'll be eliminated if I prove useless?"

She sighed. "I have so stated."

"And the others in the cell? Will they be eliminated?"

"Very probably. They will prove useless."

Z spat acidly at her, "I say the Pweetoos are worthless! They survive and spread without purpose. I also say *you're* useless! You serve useless masters!"

"There are those of my race who would agree with you," she replied, without emotion ("poker face"?). "I am programmed to serve the Pweetoos, and cannot do otherwise. *(Now THAT sounds like a phony excuse! Z thought.)*

"Now sit very still. This will take awhile. You will now be absorbing large quantities of information, so will feel some aftereffects. That is unavoidable."

She pulled down a small lever on the side of the console. Z blacked out.

When Z came to, he had a splitting headache and a head full of sounds that made no sense. He was finding it too difficult to think.

Doe asked, "How do you feel?" in a language that was very fluid and had a lot of very broad vowel sounds he had never heard before, but he did understand it. He was aware there was something he must remember. Something about Bear. He suddenly remembered.

"I'm weak. My head hurts. I need some food and rest. Please allow me to return to the cell. We can continue later," he said, in the new language.

"Very well," Doe replied. "I have used the t-machine many times, and know how it can affect the user after any intense session."

She called the guard, who led Z back to the cell. He went to the ring and attached the rope, himself. The guard tested the rope and left.

"Ape!"

Ape heard his name and swiveled his ears toward Z.

"Cripes! We have to find a way to communicate! We're all in very great danger here! We have to get out!"

"What is the matter, Z? What is happening? Are those evil Pweetoos going to kill us all, now?" came from ET.

"ET! You speak English?"

"No, Z. I can now speak Maitan. You were just speaking in Maitan. I was taught to speak and to understand Maitan by a machine. I cannot understand all. The Pweetoos say my speech centers are not very well developed for their advanced concepts. I will help. Please help me, too. I am afraid they will kill us all. I know this to be true. I do not wish to die away from my home. My spirit will never rest. I am afraid. Please. I know we can make them take us home. I do not want to wander among the stars, forever. I will not try to stop them from killing me if I am home. I am afraid. My spirit will wander. Please!"

"We're all afraid, ET," Z replied. "I will promise to do anything in my power to get us all out of this."

He looked around the group. "They've already killed Bear. We've got to form a plan!"

"Oh, no! Please! Bear was not bad, only afraid. He is dead and he never had a friend here. It is so sad!" ET said.

"He had a friend, ET. You," Z said, then paused to think for a moment, despite the headache.

"We've got to make a plan. They'll come for me soon. I told them I have to rest and eat, but they won't wait too long. We have to communicate!

"I couldn't find anything to write with here. I could draw pictures for Ape and Joe."

ET looked thoughtful. He'd been eating, and a bit of the yellow paste was in his bowl. He put a finger in and drew a line on the floor. It was dim, but visible.

"Good thinking, ET!" Z opened his panel, placed the rope across the opening and closed the lid, cutting the rope. He turned to Ape, signaling that he was to cut his rope, too.

He did.

"ET, take a grip on the ring that holds your rope."

He did.

"Now pull upward and outward while twisting the top of the ring toward Ape."

"I have seen you cut your rope, Z. I can do it."

"Now everybody, Ape, look. Everybody open their food panel again," Z ordered. They all did, and he showed them how to replace the section that was in the panel back to the piece hanging from the ring.

"Always put the section back on the ringpiece. It may prove very important. The guards will surely notice if the ropes grow shorter." Z demonstrated as he spoke. They all put the sections back and watched them "grow" together.

He went to release Thing, who ran up his leg to its now-accustomed position around his waist, with the tentacle against the side of his face. He sat next to Joe, who leaned against him. He could feel the little animal's fear.

Thing transferred to Joe, who didn't seem to mind.

"ET, we'll have to get Ape and Joe on the language machine," Z said.

"No, Z. There is no place inside their heads. It would not work. I had a spoken language. Joe has no language. Ape has no language. There is no thing to connect it. The Pweetoos said, if there is no language to connect the words, it will not work."

"It would make them understand us," Z argued.

"No, Z. There is no thing to connect. The machine makes you remember a word in Maitan for a word in your language. If you have no language, there is no word to remember. It will not work."

"I see," Z replied. "Could it teach them to read?"

"No, Z. I cannot read in Maitan because I had no written language, so there is nothing to connect. It will not work."

"I guess you're right." Z said, sighing. "Okay, everybody. Watch!"

He took a bit of the gruel on a fingertip and drew four circles, one atop the other, with the smaller one on top. He pointed to the drawing.

"Pweetoo," he said. "This is a Pweetoo. Understand?"

ET nodded. Joe pointed toward the sliding door. Ape unsheathed his claws and grinned. Thing didn't react at all.

"I don't think Thing has any intelligence," Z said. "I don't suppose we can ever communicate with it."

ET nodded.

Z took Ape's hand and looked closely into his eyes. He then pointed to the circle.

Ape nodded.

He pointed specifically to the head circle.

Ape nodded, but had a quizzical look.

Z turned back to ET. "ET, I'm going to have to use you to demonstrate something to Ape. Don't be afraid. I won't hurt you."

"Yes," ET replied.

Z turned back toward Ape, pointed to the head and said, "Pweetoo."

Ape nodded.

Z placed his hands on either side of ET's head and nodded at the circles on the floor.

Ape nodded.

Z shouted, "Ape! Now!" and swung ET's head at the wall, stopping only inches from hitting it.

Ape looked startled.

Z pointed to the figure on the floor, looking intently at Ape.

Ape nodded.

He placed his hands as though on a Pweetoo head and swung to illustrate crashing the head into the wall. He pointed to the drawing and again said, sharply, "Ape! Now!" placed his hands and swung at the wall.

Ape brightened, pointed to the figure and placed his hands as though on a head. He gave two sharp growls and swung the hands at the wall, took a foot and stomped where a body would land, then grinned at Z.

Z grinned back. "Boy! Did you ever get it!

"Okay. Now we practice getting the ropes cut all at the same time." He stood to attach his rope to Joe's ring. Joe watched him very closely.

He yelled, "Ready!" and quickly opened the food panel and reattached the severed piece. Joe studied every move.

He took Joe's hand and placed it on the ring.

"Ready!" he said.

Joe looked at him.

He pointed to the ring and made a twisting motion.

Joe rapidly opened the panel, cut the rope, reopened the panel to remove the severed piece, reattached it, reclosed the panel, and turned to Z.

Z hugged him and said, "*Very* good! A great job!" Joe was obviously pleased with the approval.

Z signaled for everyone to go to their own rings. He took Thing with him. When all were attached again, he sat on the warm floor. They all watched him carefully for awhile so he pretended to doze.

When they had relaxed, he suddenly shouted, "Ready!" and stood to release his and Thing's ropes. He replaced the cut sections and turned to find them all moving toward the door. Joe seemed very excited as Z used a finger to indicate the door was sliding upward. He pointed for Ape and ET to move to one side of the door while he and Joe went to the other.

He made a quick sign of four circles with a fingertip and moved the finger like a Pweetoo was entering the door.

He shouted, "Ape! Now!" – and nearly had heart failure when Ape grabbed ET's head and swung it violently to within an inch of the wall.

Z was standing with his hands out and his mouth hanging open. Ape looked at him and cocked his head to one side.

"If you ever do anything like that again I'll...! I thought you...! I'll...! Oh, my god!"

ET looked puzzled. "Z, what is the matter?"

"I thought you were dead! I thought Ape misunderstood my instructions, and was going to smash your head!"

"Z, Ape would never hurt me. He would never hurt any

of us. He is our friend. I trust him. He would never take any chance of hurting us."

"I know, ET. I was just surprised. It was unexpected."

He grinned largely to Ape, to show it was a good drill, then signaled for them to go back to their rings.

"We must be ready, instantly. It may be for real, next time," he warned. "ET, the whole object of this is to get a wand. We desperately need a weapon. When Ape smashes the Pweetoo's head, I want you to get the wand. Handle it very carefully. I know what it can do."

"I will try, Z. I don't know if I can touch a dead man, but I will try."

"They are *not* men, ET. They're scum! Garbage."

He sat to doze for awhile. His head felt as though it would crack open at any moment. The headache was intense. He was awakened by the door's click. Everyone sat up and tensed.

"No, it's too soon," Z said.

"Too soon." ET echoed.

The door opened. A guard came to take him back to Doe.

"I trust you are feeling well?" she asked, as he sat at the console.

"Fair," he replied. "I can stand it."

"Stand it? I don't... well, as I said earlier," she continued. "The Pweetoos need, on certain occasions, a specialized type of intelligence to solve a specific problem. This is such a time. I must determine if you are of use.

"The Pweetoos are expanding their sphere of influence and wish to lay a protective circle around the expansion. For this, they will need a much more efficient way to store and transport energy.

"You have stated you are experienced in electronic devices, both to build and to operate them."

She checked her notes. "Would you be able to find such a method?"

"I can solve any problem, given time and information," Z replied. "No doubt, you'll have much to teach me about their present system. You *will* supply the tools I'll need?"

"Approximately how long will the learning phase take, in your estimation?" she asked.

"I can't say," he answered, exasperated. "I don't have the information, yet. I'll have to learn the technological details first. You must consider that these things are many centuries advanced over what I know."

"We can give you the knowledge. The information is in the machine."

"It's my turn to ask a question, now," Z said. "I've been thinking about the caste system of the Pweetoos. It seems to me they're totally regimented and extremely over-specialized. I've heard you say they're bred for doing certain types of tasks, such as piloting this ship.

"What are they?"

"The Pweetoos are from a planet near a double sun." she replied. "Far back in their race's evolution, one of the suns became unstable and began radiating in sudden bursts that made it difficult to live on the surface. The ancestors of the race already were well-adapted to underground existence, so they survived. The civilization was, necessarily, quite highly structured, as there was no room or sustenance for any individuals that could serve no immediate purpose. The larvae are trained from the earliest stages for a specific task. When they become adults, they are ready to step into their role without further delay.

"Some methods are used to vastly increase certain abilities through feeding of specialized nutrients. The eggs demonstrate characteristics that make it rare to train an individual for a task it cannot complete."

Z was staring at her.

"Eggs? Larvae? Specific characteristics? Feeding...?

"Great god! They're *insects*! *Cockroaches*! They're

something like desert termites!" he laughed. "They have a single queen who lays all the eggs, right?"

"Well...," Doe stammered. "They do, uh, that is, they have brood mothers, one on each planet they use for, uh...."

Z shook his head. "So! And why do you seem to be so structured?"

He also wondered why she always seemed so phony, like she was play-acting to impress him.

"I thought we were to discuss Pweetoos, not Immins," she replied. "However, when a mammalian race reaches a certain point in scientific development, it discovers the basic traits and the genetic reasons for them. They soon learn to manipulate those traits. It becomes inevitable that, after a certain time, a government or dictator will begin to produce citizens to fit into specific areas. Soon, the result is a race as structured as the Pweetoos became naturally. Such a process further stabilizes the race in the way the Pweetoos are naturally stabilized. Anything else is unstable, and will not survive."

"You're saying the Maitans were unstable? Come *on*!"

The Maitans were a special evolutionary case that would not be discussed. Z felt she had already said more than she was allowed, and might get in trouble. It also seemed a bit phony, as everything concerning her seemed to be. Her claims that she was bred to act in a certain capacity was definitely false. She couldn't be here, asking these questions, if it were true.

"I think you tend to confuse stability and stagnation," Z said. "What purpose do your precious Pweetoos serve?

"You speak of races that have no use. I say the Pweetoos have no use! Survival for the sake of survival is pointless. What purpose does stability serve? Why bother?"

Doe sat staring at the floor through this with just the hint of a smirk. Odd.

"Your Pweetoos serve no purpose. They're destructive and are a sore on the face of the galaxy. They're useless. You serve useless masters, so are yourself useless."

She looked up at him. "Perhaps what you say is true. You must realize that I am bred and programmed only to serve the Pweetoos. I can do no other."

"We must now get back to the problem at hand. Let us now determine if you are to be of use."

She shuffled through her notes and read one sheet. He noted the sly little look she gave him.

"Are you qualified to redesign and build the added power storage facilities the Pweetoos seek?"

"Of course," Z sneered. "All I have to do is catch up on fifty centuries of scientific exploration, learn to use the tools of the Maitans, develop a few-odd centuries worth of technology, pick up a couple hundred years of technique and, Voila! It's done!"

He leered at her. "You can arrange that, of course?"

"Certainly," she replied. "The needed information is in the machine. We will begin immediately. I will set the machine for your education. Place the headgear. There will, of course, be the unpleasant effects from the more intense session, as you have already experienced. That is unavoidable."

"One moment!" Z demanded. "My friends in the cell are to be well-treated. I need them."

"They are useless. They will be eliminated," she replied, offhandedly. "Place the helmet."

"Oh, no! If I don't have them, I can't work! It's a strong psychological thing with my race!"

"That is not true. You have no need of them."

"Let's put it this way, then," Z snarled. "If they're not well-treated, I won't solve your problem – and *you* will have failed, in the eyes of the Pweetoos. I'll make it very plain my lack of cooperation is due to solely *your* attitude!"

She thought a moment, then said, "I will see they are kept unharmed."

"You'd better! I'm not bluffing!" He placed the helmet and blacked out.

When he regained consciousness, he had the headache, so Doe allowed him to return to the holding cell to rest and eat. When the guard left, the rest of the group wanted to know what had happened.

"I got a hell of a lot of useful information about energy and power supplies. It includes all types of weapons, computers and dimensions and a lot of things I've never dreamed about!

"I've also got the most intense headache I've ever had. I have to sleep. I can't think. My mind's all jumbled.

"Just be ready to act. We don't have much more time."

ET questioned their ability to pilot the ship.

"Any of us can pilot the ship. The machines can teach us how. They, apparently, can teach us almost anything.

"How'd you like to be a space pilot, ET?"

"I will do whatever is necessary to get home."

"We may have to make a stop or two before home, but I'm sure we'll get there, now," Z answered. He laid back against the wall and said, "Be ready to act with no further notice. It's important."

He began to drift off to sleep, and felt Thing wrap around him. He remembered thinking it odd.

He drifted on the fringes of sleep for a few minutes. His body seemed to be asleep, his eyes and ears were asleep, but his mind was not. He'd never experienced anything like it. The headache was intense, but seemed to be some-where over there, while his thoughts were over here. Displaced. There was an area of warmth. It was Thing. He knew that, but didn't know why he knew it, and didn't care.

He was walking along the Sarasota beach again. He was awakening with a white rope around his waist. He was watching, noting, seeing, remembering things he hadn't been aware of at the time. Joe was pleading with him. ET was nodding knowingly. Ape was grinning the toothy grin. Zeekou was jumping up and down in frustration. Eerf was screaming at him.

There were all those words that didn't make any sense in his head. There were diagrams, new terms and currents flowing and curling backward on themselves, moving in two different directions in two places that were the same place. He didn't know what it meant, yet he did.

ET's head slamming toward the wall. Ape was grinning again.

It was wrong! Wrong! Wrong!

There was some kind of question and the knowledge that the method was wrong, but the only way. Thing was speaking in the voice in the helmet, saying it would find a way to help him, but would be damned to hell, if it did.

Diagrams again of the awesome power spheres the ships used the education machines had taught him about and the Maitans screaming in pain and humiliation.

The Maitans were in the power spheres! They were alive!

Thing was telling them to wait. Stars flying by with people of all kinds, pleading for his help, but he was moving too fast! He would reach for them, but they were soon lost in the growing distance. Forty one. *Forty one!* Dead! All dead! *Double!*

He was sinking, sinking.

Termite hills, and Doe. She was sitting in a black chair, a rocking chair. She was knitting gloves for the Pweetoos and was grinning to herself. The hills were growing bigger and bigger and there were lines of ants carrying food into the mounds. Doe was giving the gloves to the ants that brought the fattest morsels, which she popped into her mouth, then went back to rocking and knitting.

The mounds were made of stars glued together. The food was living people, wriggling and crying out as they were carried to the queen.

He had promised! He had promised! He had promised!

There was help, but it was all putty and he must shape it or it couldn't help him. It was crying to him to free it! If he could free the help, it would save them all.

There was the comforting warmth that was, somehow, Thing, tightly wrapped around him.

He slept. Deep, black, restful sleep.

When Z awakened later, all the others seemed to still be asleep, but as soon as he moved, Thing woke up and put the tentacle against the side of his face. He noticed Thing was attached to his ring.

"How'd you get here?" he asked, as he stroked the little animal.

"Ape brought it over," ET said, from his spot.

"I thought you were asleep," Z said.

"I was. I heard you talk to Thing. I always wake up to sounds. To little sounds. I am a very light sleeper."

"We'd better make some kind of plan, ET. So far, we're barely prepared to get out of this room.

"We've seen six guards. I have to assume there are at least six interrogators, because we were all out of this room at the same time. In addition, there are at least two other special interrogators I've seen, myself, at various times. Someone prepares the food and does maintenance, and at least one feeder.

"There are at least eighteen. I don't think we have to worry much about any, except the guards. These things are so specialized they can't function at any but the tasks they were bred for.

"It's best we get one guard, take the wand, and either out think or overpower the rest. We must have room to move.

"I know that's not much of a plan, but we don't know enough to plan any further. Doing nothing is suicide. We may not have a chance in a million, if we act, but we don't have any chance at all if we don't!

"What do you think?"

"I will do anything you ask, Z. A small chance with you is better than no chance without you. I do not think you would do anything to harm us. You care even about Thing, who is not of your race and who may not even be intelligent. It should be nothing to you, yet you protect it. You care. Pweetoos do not. They feel nothing. I am no longer afraid of them, I just pity them. They have no purpose or reason to exist. They have no spirit. When they die, it is as though they never were. It is sad."

"ET, you are very perceptive. You see deeply into the souls of others, even to seeing when they have no soul.

"You trust. I hope you're never again hurt by your trust, but have to say you trust too much. Ape could easily have killed you when we practiced the attack by the door. He doesn't have the intelligence to realize how strong he is or how weak the rest of us are.

"I don't mean to say he would hurt you on purpose, only that he could do unbelievable damage by accident, not ever wanting to."

"No, Z. Please listen. Ape is very intelligent, he just thinks different thoughts. His people do not talk, which is why he does not talk. I think his home is a very alone place. I think he is never with others. He sees in you a leader, and he will follow you. You are hope. I do not think he has taken an order from anyone. Not ever. He will take orders from you. You give us hope."

He looked at Z and shook his head. "I am sorry. I would not want to be you, here and now. You have made us all your responsibility. You promised to save us. We did not know the words, but we all do understand. You are honest, and will do as you promised. You will die, if you must, but you will save us. You will make a plan, and we will do what you say. If you do not save us, your spirit will wander. You will say you do not believe this, but you know it is true. You cannot let us down. It is a thing inside of you that made you give your promise. It is a thing inside of you that will make you keep the promise. You feel and you care. You cry inside for Joe. Joe is afraid, but

Joe will do your plan to be good enough for you. Thing perhaps has no mind, but will hold to you. You will protect it, even if it means you will die. You will keep your promise, because you cannot not keep it."

"Damn it, ET! You make me...!" The door clicked.

"Ready!" Z shouted.

It was amazing how quickly everyone cut the ropes and moved to the door. They arrived at their places just as it began to open. The guards entered.

"Ape! No!" Z shouted, but it was too late. Ape grabbed the first guard and smashed its head into the wall.

"No! There are too many!" Z shouted, as ET dove at the legs of the second guard, hitting it from behind, just as Joe hit it from the front, taking a jolt from the wand as he hit. The guard went down, and Ape stamped the head against the floor and wrenched away the wand. Z hit the third guard and took a hit from the wand as he hit it. The guard was down, but so was Z. He was on the floor, trying to get up past the pain.

The guard jumped to its feet and came toward him with the wand held like a sword, ready to run him through. Suddenly, four strong tentacles came around from behind the guard's head, covering the eyes, ear and nose slits.

The guard dropped the wand and reached up with a claw to cut a deep gash in a tentacle, just as Z staggered to his feet. Thing made a mewling sound, but tightened its grip.

Z was bent over from pain, but managed to clasp both hands together. He slammed the sides of the clasped hands into the guard between the head and second segments in a power chop. The head lolled to the side and the guard fell, obviously dead.

Z grabbed Thing and carefully peeled the tentacles loose from the guard's head. Thing clung to him and continued the mewling sounds.

"Calm down, little guy. We'll fix it. Take it easy," he

said. "Little fellow, I never expected any help from you, and you saved my life! None of us have any right to be alive right now! There were too many. We only practiced for one!"

ET took Thing and was petting and trying to calm it. Ape was petting Joe and had him calmed down. Z knew what the little animal was suffering from that wand! He had been hit hard. Twice. And he was used to physical pain.

ET looked up at Z.

"When you said, 'Ape! No!' Ape thought you said 'Ape! Now!' and did as we practiced. I knew I could not get the wand. It was too late to stop and I did not know what to do. Joe was running to the other guard, so I ran into the other side. Joe was very brave. He knew he would be touched by the wand, and he saw the wand knock Ape down. He did it, anyhow. He did it for you. He would do anything for you. I did not think Thing was intelligent, but I now think it is only different. It is from a different kind of world. It figured the guard would kill you and it figured how to stop the guard. It does not think like I do, but it hurts like I do. I think it is hurt more than we know. I think we must stop it from losing fluid. We must help it."

Ape came over and dropped two of the wands and their power packs on the floor beside Z. He went to the last guard and twisted the power pack off. It came away with a piece of the guard's head still attached.

Z took off his shirt and tore a strip, which he tied around the wound on the tentacle. It seemed to stop the bleeding, but Thing let it hang.

"All right, heroes!" Z called. "We've started it and, after a terrible take-off, we're in the air. We're ahead of the game, right now, but there's no turning back. The die is cast, and all those other silly cliché's. Now, we have to plan where we go from here. We have to take over this ship.

"I know most of you can't understand me, but I think better out loud, when I'm under pressure."

"I will explain to Ape and Joe what we must do. I think I can. We have made some sign language," ET suggested. "I think I know what we must do."

"Good!" Z answered. "We have to clean this place up, now. It wouldn't do to have anyone come in and find a bunch of dead guards laying around.

"I noticed the feeder would touch a little light along here to open a panel he threw the bowls and leftovers in. It touched this one."

Z touched the light, but nothing happened.

ET said, "The guards wear rings. I noticed, when they touch a light, they touch it with the ring. The ring is what opens things, I think."

"Good thinking, ET. I'm glad you're a good observer," Z replied as he checked the guards' hands. They all wore small rings with odd-shaped crystals mounted on them. The rings seemed glued to their fingers, as the boxes were glued to the heads of the guards.

He picked up a wand and touched it to a ring. The crystal shattered.

"That sure ain't it!" he said.

Ape grabbed another of the guards and drug it over to a ring in the wall. He opened the panel, inserted the guard's finger and closed the lid. It cut the finger off, then he reopened the panel and handed Z the ring, finger and all.

Z touched the ring to the light and the panel opened. It was about two feet high by three wide. He leaned a little into the panel and looked in. There was a strange glowing grid in the bottom.

He signaled for Ape to bring the guard's body with the missing finger over and drop it in.

Ape pushed the body into the panel and Z touched the light to close it. He waited a moment, then reopened the panel and leaned in. There was a slight smell of ozone, but the panel was just as before – empty, with a glowing grid on the bottom.

Z shoved the guard's body with the shattered ring crystal in, while Ape cut the finger off the last one. Ape brought the last body over and disposed of it.

"Great disposal! No stains, no muss, no fuss! Just throw in the garbage and flush!"

He looked around the room again.

"All right. We open the doors with the wands as well as protect ourselves. We open the disposals with the rings.

"I don't suppose we can hope to use the wands to force any information from the Pweetoos. They're much too specialized to help. Maybe we can use them on Doe, or maybe not. I don't like the idea."

Everyone was watching attentively as he said, "Okay, ET. I'm going out. I'll see how soon I come across some of the crew of this ship. I'll take a wand and you and Ape or Joe take the others. I'll keep one ring and you take the other."

He picked up a wand, and found the power pack would fit in his pocket and still have enough line to reach his outstretched arm's length. He dropped a finger with its ring into the other pocket.

"I'll close the door when I go out. You've all seen how the guards open and close the doors, so you'll know how to get out if anything happens to me. You all know the procedure if a guard should show up. If there's more than one, be very careful. I'm sure there won't be more than three.

"You can tie yourselves and hide the wands behind you. Wait until they're close enough so you can't miss to zap them. Work out a signal so you'll all strike at once. If one or more are out of range, you'll lose the element of surprise and will find yourselves in serious trouble. If there are too many or if they're not in a position where you can get to all of them at once, you'll be safer to wait.

"I plan to return, soon. Don't take any chances. It's better to wait and do nothing than to be wrong.

"Please! I can't tell you enough. Be very careful!

"Okay, everybody. ET's in charge.

"ET, I hope you can communicate well enough to make them understand."

ET held out a hand, which Z took.

"Yes, Z. I'm sure I can. You will be the one with the most danger, so you must be most careful, too. For our sakes. If you are not here, we are lost. We cannot use the machines because we cannot read nor be taught to read. Be very careful. We will worry until you return."

"I'll be careful, ET," Z promised. "I don't know how I get myself into these situations, but I'm sure we can win, now. We have the upper hand.

"I'm gone."

He went out and closed the door, but immediately reopened it and leaned in to say, "ET, keep a close watch on thing. I believe it's more serious than we know, so keep an eye on it, guys."

"I do not understand," ET said.

"Thing," Z said. "I think its injuries are far more serious than we know."

"But I cannot place my eye on Thing! I cannot see if it is not in my head!"

"It's an idiom, an expression!" Z cried. "It means keep a close watch on Thing!"

"I understand," ET replied. "Please do not use idioms. They confuse me."

"Right, ET. I'm sorry," Z said. As he went out again, he mumbled, "*Don't* use idioms! They can't understand the damned things! Sheesh!"

He stopped just outside and watched as the door closed.

He listened very carefully for awhile. There was no sound, and the feeling was eerie, in the extreme. It was like the non-sound in an empty house with a refrigerator running in another room, humming just below audibility.

A plan. There must be some kind of plan – even if it's as bad as the one that almost got them all killed a few minutes ago in that room. Go in a definite direction, observe every detail. Find what those symbols mean, if anything. Find signs – and *don't* get caught!

Standing there would solve nothing.

As Z moved from the door, he took careful note of the mark on its outer side. It was a hexagon.

The next mark to the left was a triangle superimposed over a square. He went to the door on the right where, he noted a triangle with a line across it.

"That's easy enough. We're in suite six," he muttered. It was now obvious, as he had noted a square before, that one just counted the points. No doubt, number one would be a dot.

He walked ahead into the curved hall. He was moving to his left as he left room six and the hall curved right. He was moving clockwise around a circle.

He passed a square, then a triangle. A line followed, then a dot. Right! Just as he figured.

He could read Maitan, so these geometric symbols were just a representation for the numbers.

Because the Pweetoos didn't know Maitan numbers?

That simply couldn't be! It must be so other races could be taught. Maybe races like ET, who could speak Maitan, but who couldn't read.

Why would a Pweetoo care?

Maybe they reacted to symbols, themselves. Maybe those guards couldn't be taught anything more complicated. Maybe, when the Pweetoos copied the ship, they copied what the original builder had on the doors. Maybe it didn't mean a damned thing, anyhow! Move on!

Across from the dot was the only door he found on that side of the hall. It had an interlooping set of three circles. This was the ship's center, judging from the curved hall. Engine or something.

The following door had a square with two bright triangles super-imposed over it, tip to base. Four plus three plus three equals ten.

He walked back around to the hexagon and stopped, thought a moment, and walked around the hallway from directly across from six to where he was back at the same spot, his left shoulder brushing the wall, mumbling just below audibility, "Twenty one long strides. About sixty to sixty five feet. That would make the inner circle about twenty feet across. The hall is maybe ten feet wide. The rooms I've been in are all about twenty feet deep and are cutoff pie shapes with curved inner and outer walls. That's a circle about eighty feet across at the outer walls of the rooms. There were cubicles behind some of the rooms. I don't know how big they are."

He reached to try to measure the height of the hall.

"Eleven feet, more or less. The rooms are maybe eight and a half. That means the height increases toward the center and the ship is round and, oh, for the...! It's a flying saucer! And I always said the people who saw those things were loopy! I'll be totally damned!"

Supermarket tabloid sheet time again! He could see the big headlines: "I wanted to make out with a girl, but I made it out of the solar system!" average American male claims. Kidnapped by evil aliens from Betelgeuse, man makes daring escape. Saves the universe! (Story pg. 23)

He grinned to himself. Even now, he knew all those stories were nothing but hallucinations and fictions. This, unfortunately, was not! If he didn't keep his mind on what he was doing, he could end up dead!

He couldn't help being surprised he had seen no one, thus far.

He went back to the inner door with the three circles. He stood to one side of the door and touched the symbol with the wand tip. Nothing happened.

"What the hell?!"

Well, there were three buttons, and they certainly weren't there for decoration!

He pushed the green button, then touched the symbol and watched as a small spark shot to the door.

"A spark. That must be the one that hurts. I wish we'd tested them before I left the guys with no way to know what to do."

He considered going back and telling ET, but decided ET probably had the sense to test the wands, and he hadn't seen anyone, anyhow. To get to room six, they'd have to come into the hall. No one had.

He pushed the black button and touched the symbol. The door opened, revealing a room about four by six feet. There was a symbol on each wall.

On his left was a triangle, red tip pointing downward. On the rear wall was an "X" with a circle around it. A sign in Maitan under it said, "To enter here without protection is slow and painful death."

He mumbled, "That seems clear enough. Left door is a down stair, right door is an up stair – and the back door is a stairway to hell – probably the engine room. Maybe it's radioactive, but what I learned from the machine says there isn't much danger."

Now a moment to consider which stairway to take. It occurred to him the ship might not be a saucer, and all the Pweetoos and Immins were on other floors. Logically, the bridge would be on the top of the ship. That would be the place to go before he was discovered – while he still had the element of surprise on his side. He may soon desperately need that small edge! If this was a multilayered ship, there may be hundreds of bugs aboard!

Standing there wouldn't help.

He tapped the left wall with the wand, black button down, of course.

For a long moment nothing else happened and he was considering the orange button, when the back door suddenly opened. He felt a moment's panic, then noticed there were no doors on the sides, only the symbols.

"Ah! Elevator, not stairs!"

He went in and the door closed. A moment later the back door opened.

The place the door opened onto was a flat white metal floor with no adornment whatever. It was covered by a clear dome. The covering was only about five feet high where he entered, so he had to stoop over to enter at all. It went to about nine feet in the center.

He went to the center. It was a strange feeling. He took a deep breath, then looked up to see stars. Lots of them. Some were close – one was the apparent diameter of about one third the full moon of Earth, and was a dull red color.

He looked to the sides and saw he was right about the saucer shape. The ship sloped away from him on all sides and was about a hundred fifty feet across.

This was obviously not the bridge. It wasn't even used, if appearances were any indication.

"Big," he remarked, and went back to the elevator, where he touched the down triangle with the wand tip. He noticed the wall where he originally entered had the three circle symbol.

The back door opened again.

"Uh-oh!"

The room he was looking into was the same size as the one he just left. Fine.

It also had a clear dome. Fine.

There was a great deal of very complicated machinery in the room, and several consoles, one of which had a Pweetoo sitting (?) at it. The Pweetoo had on an extremely complicated headgear. Also fine.

The problem was that he was upside down in relation to the room. The floor was just "above" his head!

He closed his mouth and glanced upward, or downward, in this case, through the dome. There were a lot of stars on this side, but none so close.

"Okay, so we're in space and we have artificial gravity. Neat, but how do I get aligned to the room? This is sorta disconcerting."

He searched around the door frame and found several small indentations on a little silvery plaque toward one side. The indentations looked familiar, with an odd shape, and were quite small. They were the size and shape of the crystals on....

He remembered the ring and took it from his pocket. One of the indentations was the shape and size of the crystal. Other uses for the rings, too, it would seem!

He placed the crystal into the indentation and watched a light come on behind it. He waited awhile, but nothing more happened.

It must just be a ready light. Do something else.

He pressed the ring into the socket, but nothing changed.

He twisted the ring and the socket turned. So did the elevator. He had soon turned the elevator completely around, while the gravity stayed at his feet.

He aligned the elevator to the room and went in.

He inspected several of the consoles and was ignored by the Pweetoo. It seemed oblivious of his existence as it simply sat, unmoving, watching the console before it.

Z walked over to stand close behind the Pweetoo, where he could inspect the console board. It was obviously the pilot's console.

Time to try to get some kind of rise out of the pilot!

"Looks complicated," he said.

The Pweetoo ignored him.

He tapped the helmet. The Pweetoo stared at him a few seconds, the same way the others stared at him when he had them confused, then turned back to the console, where it threw up a lever and pushed it into its socket several times, then ignored Z's attempts to get its attention.

"I'm not part of what you're bred to deal with, so that's that!" Z mumbled. He wandered over to another console and was studying the writings on the dials and switches when he heard a click. He looked to see the elevator door as it closed.

"Oh, hell! I'm gonna have company!"

He should have thought of that one! The pilot wouldn't be equipped to handle some alien prisoner on the bridge, so would call a specialist! A guard! Surprise time!

It was up to him to start a war of wands. He had the one fact in his favor, besides the surprise angle. He knew there weren't many of them, if this ship was a saucer – but, of course, one could be too many!

He stood close to the elevator doorway and waited. Soon the door opened and a Pweetoo guard came into the room. Z jumped in front of it and slapped it between the eyes, green button down. Nothing happened, except the guard pointed to the elevator with its own wand.

Z said, "Oh, holy shit!" and marched into the elevator. He stopped in the entrance for a second to place the ring in the socket, then swiftly turned to very carefully hit the guard's ring finger with his wand as he twisted the ring. The elevator began turning as he hit the three circle symbol with the black button pushed. The door closed before the guard reacted.

"I hope I got the ring! It can't get down without it!"

It could, but would be upside down, but maybe that

wouldn't matter to it. One thing was sure! He'd soon know!

As soon as the door opened he ran to suite six, slapped the symbol with the wand and the door opened. He ran into the room past the group, who were in the attack position they had practiced.

"Oh, god! I'm glad no guards came while I was away!" he cried. "ET, the wands don't work on the Pweetoos. We can't use them in defense. The ants will probably come for me, soon. We have to change our plans. We can't use the wands.

"Oh, god! I had planned to get the upper hand when we had wands! That's a dead issue. The wands are useless – and you guys were here with no defense!"

"Z, please be calm. We have excellent defense. We have Ape. He is more than any Pweetoo. If we cannot use the wands, we can beat them the way we already did. Ape is as many Pweetoos in strength and all of us can move quickly, here, and the Pweetoos cannot. The floor is too smooth. Please do not worry about us, Z. We have a small plan. We are more safe than are you. We are here in a place we know and we can have a plan. Out there, there is no plan, because we do not yet know what is there. Ape will protect us here."

Z answered, "But I was counting on these wands! I thought they'd make us as well-armed as the guards!"

"Please be calm. We do not need wands while we have Ape. We already have a plan we know will work. We must be more careful and you must not again allow a guard to touch you with its wand. Thing cannot help you again. I know we can win. Be calm."

Z went cold all over.

"What do you mean? Why can't Thing help? Is it dea ... if anything happens to Thing, I'll never forgive myself! Thing saved my life!"

Z went to Thing, who was limp. It made a motion to reach him. Joe was holding it and looked worriedly at Z.

"I think it is very sick. I think it will die. It is not your fault, Z. Do not blame yourself for these things over which you have no control. You are not to blame now. There is nothing to do. It is unlike us, and we don't know what to do. Thing is from a different world than we know. We do not know what to do. Thing knows we care very much about it, and that is what is important. It will die knowing that we care and that it has shown that it cares. Its spirit will stay close. We will never be apart. Our spirits will be sure Thing's spirit does not wander the stars. It will always be with those who care."

"It is *not* going to die!" Z cried. "I promised to take it home and I am, by god, taking it home! It is *not* going to die! It is going to be alive and well!"

He went to the door and hit it with the wand. "ET, tell Ape the wands are as much as useless!" he ordered, then ran to the interrogation room, where he left Doe, opened the door and went directly to the back. He hit the symbol on the door there with the wand and it opened, revealing Doe, sitting on a bench with a helmet on. Z tapped the helmet.

Doe looked up at him and removed the helmet. She waited.

"Doe, I need your help," he said. She stared at him.

He shook her shoulder. "Did you hear me?"

"Of course. What do you want?" she asked.

"Where can I get medical attention?"

"How were you hurt?" she asked, looking him over.

"It isn't for me. Thing is hurt."

"What thing? You make no sense!"

"No, Doe. Thing is the little gray tentacled animal," he explained.

"It cannot be harmed. There is no danger within the

bounds of its tether."

"Doe, I'm not tied. We're all untied. Thing is badly hurt."

"That is not possible," she said, calmly. "Why do you have a wand? The guards do not allow prisoners to have wands."

"I'm not going to argue with you!" Z yelled. "I personally have nothing against you, but I won't allow Thing to die! I'll use this wand on you, if necessary."

He waved the wand at her. "Get some medical care personnel here, and I mean right *now*!"

"There are no medical personnel. The medical machines can do all that is necessary. Place the animal in the machine and I will set the controls," she said, resignedly, as she stood.

"I'll be right back! Have the machine ready."

Z ran back to six, where he grabbed the comatose little animal into his arms. "ET, get everyone to come with me!" he said, as he ran from the room. ET waved for Ape and Joe to come and ran out behind Z. When they were back in the room with Doe, she pointed to a box where she had opened a bench by lifting the seat.

"Place the animal into the box and affix the helmet," she instructed.

Z found a small wire helmet in the box and quickly put it on Thing's "head." The eyes were in the way, but bent to the sides. Thousands of very fine white filaments came out of the sides of the box and contacted every part of Thing's body.

"Close the medbox," Doe ordered. "It will cycle and will reopen automatically after treatment.

"I am studying. Please do not again disturb me."

She set some controls on the console and went back into her cubicle. The door closed.

Z was really amazed she was so calm about all of them just running around the ship with wands, but she seemed to take it as a normal matter of course. She must be as programmed as the Pweetoos. She had no instructions as to how to deal with the situation, so she ignored it!

So why did this seem a little overdone – like an act? Why was she so openly smirking when he first went to her room?

Z heard ET yell, "Ape! Now!" and a crash. He spun around to see Ape tearing the power pack from the head of a dead guard. Ape grinned to Z, who grinned back.

Ape handed the power pack and wand to Joe and twisted the ring finger off. He handed the finger to Z, picked up the Pweetoo body and shrugged. Z searched the wall until he found a disposal panel beside Doe's door. Ape brought the body over and dumped it into the panel, then turned with his toothy grin.

Z looked around the group. "That should leave two guards to go," he said.

ET was by the door. "Here they come now."

Z signaled for everyone to get close against the wall on either side of the door. Ape stood closest to the door on one side, while Z took the close position on the other, then they waited.

No one entered, so Z cautiously went out. "Yai! Oh, my god!" he exclaimed, "There were three of them! They went on by!

"Trouble! There are more than I thought. We'll have to see where they go.

"ET, you keep Joe here with you and watch for Thing to be finished on the machine. If anyone comes, hide.

"Come on, Ape!" he signaled for Ape to come with him. As he went out, he said, "Close the door, ET."

Z and Ape stayed just around the curve of the hall from the guards and saw them open a door to enter a room. Z then checked the symbol on the door. It was a straight line, triangle and square.

"Nine," he said. "Okay, Ape. Back to the conference."

He waved for Ape to come along, and they went back to the instruction room. They entered to find no one was there!

"They're gone!" he cried.

"We are here. You said to hide if anyone came, so we are hiding. We did not know it would be you and Ape." ET and Joe got out from under the lid of a large bench.

"You are back very soon. Did you find the guards? How many are there? Must we have a new plan? How long will Thing be in here? I am sorry. I have many questions and few answers."

"I have a sort of plan, ET," Z replied. "I think I can call all the guards from the console here on the instructor board. I imagine Doe called the one who came here before she went back to her room. If I can call them one at the time, we can defeat them with ease."

Z studied the controls on the console. He found a set of levers along one side with symbols beside them that matched the ones on the doors. There were several extra symbols.

"I have to find what these mean! I thought it would be so easy!" he cried in exasperation.

Every corner they came to that seemed to be on the road out had some kind of roadblock on it.

How corny! Think of the problem and stop letting your mind wander all over the place. Think!

"Can you not read the Maitan? What is the problem? I begin to become nervous again. Does everything go wrong now? Did the machine not instruct you properly? If you cannot work with the machine, can we find another way?"

"I can read it, ET," Z answered. "The problem is that there are too many symbols. I dare not use the machine until I know what these other things are for. I may call up more than I ever bargained for!

"You got any ideas?"

ET thought a moment. "I think so, Z. Do you remember that Doe is in another room? Perhaps those symbols are for those rooms. Did you consider that? Is there a mark on the machine for Doe's room? Maybe there are marks for other things, and only some of them are for the guards? Maybe some will call the interrogators?"

"Good thinking!" Z said, snapping his fingers. "There are definitely symbols for each room, ET. There were just too many. There are ten outer rooms and the domes and the elevator and the engine room. Maybe each cubicle has its own symbol."

He went to the rear door and checked for a symbol. It was there, naturally. He had tapped it to open the door earlier, but had been much too concerned about Thing to remember it.

He went back to the main console. The mark was there. One roadblock that was a mirage.

Oh, brother! Cliché time! *Bad* cliché time!

"You're right again, ET," he remarked. "I don't know what happens to my mind, sometimes. I think I go into underdrive, rather than overdrive."

"What are you saying, Z? I do not understand you. What is underdrive?"

"Nothing, ET. It was a joke I played on the Pweetoos."

He checked all the symbols on the console.

"Let's see. There are four extra marks. The mark for Doe's room is just before the mark for this one, so we have four cubicles, and we know where they are.

"There's a symbol for the observation dome and the pilot's dome and, yes, even one for the elevator. The one for the engine room is green.

"Yeah, they're all here. There's one with all the symbols printed very small in a semicircle around it. I assume that's the P.A."

He studied the board for a moment, then shook his head.

"Is there a problem, Z? Perhaps I can help. I sometimes see things others miss. I see details that are not important at the time, but are sometimes important, later. What is the problem? Is it a thing I can help with?"

"You're just telling me politely that I'm addled. You don't have to be polite. I know it," Z replied. "Our problem is that I can call any room I choose or, at least, turn on the call.

"I don't speak into the microphone. The pilot didn't when it called the guard. All it did ... of course! It pushed the switch down!

"I suppose you'd push it once for one guard and more for others.

"Okay! Ready! Battle stations, everyone!

"You stay with me at the console, ET. It'll give the guard something to look at when it comes in."

He waved for Ape to go to one side of the door and Joe to the other, then depressed switch nine.

They waited. About a minute and a half later, a guard came into the door. It stopped just inside and stared at Z and ET. They waited a few seconds, without anyone moving and Z said, "What the hell?! Get it, Ape!"

ET yelled, "Ape! Now!"

Ape grabbed the guard's head and smashed it into the wall. Joe grabbed the wand and held it out, while Ape ripped the box from the guard's head. He handed the box to Joe, twisted the finger with the ring off, picked the body up, went to the wall panel where Joe placed the ring against the light, dumped the body in and Joe closed the door.

He turned and grinned at Z, who grinned back.

"Efficient as all hell! Brutal, but effective," Z mumbled.

"Z, do not be angry with Ape. He did not know to attack, unless you said to. It was what we practiced. He needed the signal, and he did as you told him to. It is not fair to be angry with him. He did only what we said was the right thing to do, and we taught him with the signal."

"I'm definitely not angry, ET. I'm damned glad we have the control. I was muttering because it's necessary for us to be so violent. I don't like violence."

There was a loud "Clack!" behind them. "What the hell?!" Z cried, as he spun to see the lid from Thing's bench sprung open. He ran over, looked in and laughed in relief as four tentacles came from the box to wrap tightly around his neck and shoulders. Joe ran over and Thing wrapped a tentacle around him, too.

"I've never been so relieved in my entire life, little fellow!" Z cried. "You scared the living hell out of me! I've been running around with a knot in my stomach so ... I couldn't live with myself, if anything happened to you.

"You've missed a bit, but our problems are much less now."

Z walked over to the console and looked at it a moment. Thing was sitting on his shoulder.

"Thing, I'm so glad you're well. I was so afraid for you, but couldn't say anything. Z was too worried, already," ET said.

Thing reached to place a tentacle around his neck, then reached to Ape to do the same.

"One for all!" Z said, "I can't call another guard here. It would seem strange for them to keep coming here and nobody goes back."

"Z, it would make no difference. The guards do not think. If you call them, they come. Nothing is strange to them. They simply do what they are told. If they are bred for it. Call them. They will come. It is what they do. They have no other duty. It will not be strange to them. They do not think."

"You're right, ET. Sometimes you make me feel just plain stupid."

Z pushed the switch for nine and depressed it. He waved Ape to the door, Joe came over and had Thing transfer to him before going to his side of the door.

They waited. No guard came.

"Now what?!" Z exclaimed.

"Perhaps they have a number. You have called number one, so it cannot answer you. Try to call some other numbers."

"That's right, ET! The pilot pressed the switch a couple of times," Z said, pressing the switch twice.

None came. He pressed it three times. Nothing.

"That's not it. I'm not getting anything."

"Z, we have already killed five of the guards. Perhaps we are calling numbers for dead guards. Please keep trying. It is the only thing we have to make them come only one at the time. We have to keep trying a little more."

"You're right again, ET."

He pushed the switch four times. Nothing.

Five times. A guard came and was taken care of.

None came on numbers six or seven and one came on eight. He continued until twelve, with no further results.

"I think that takes care of the guards, ET," Z mused "Our next problem is to get the rest of the Pweetoos."

The door to Doe's cubicle opened and she came into the room to stare at them.

"It is time to begin work on the power storage problem," she started, then again stared around at the others. "What are these creatures doing here? Surely the medical procedures are completed. They were to be returned to the cell. They will go there immediately. Now! I have no time to waste on these worthless creatures.

"Go! Now! I will see they are eliminated if they resist!"

She went to the console, threw switch nine and depressed it several times. Z sat on a bench to wait with her. After a couple of minutes, she went back to the console and held the switch down for about fifteen seconds.

"The guards will all come, now. Your useless creatures will suffer for this useless defiance! I will see to it!" she said, haughtily. "I will not be defied!"

"The guards are all dead. They aren't coming," Z said. "The plans are changed. I'm not building a power storage or anything else for the Pweetoos. I'm going home. We're taking this ship over. We're in charge, now. We're going to eliminate your dear useless Pweetoos."

Doe stared at him a moment, looked around the room, went into her cubicle, and closed the door. Ape started after her.

"No, Ape. Let her think it over," Z said, and waved for Ape to follow him.

"ET, we're going to check the halls. We'll be right back. While we're gone, you and Joe study this room very carefully. Learn where everything is and how to use anything you can, but be very careful. Don't forget, there's a lot we don't know about this ship or who else is on it. There were Doe and the Pweetoos. There could easily be others of other races."

He and Ape left to check the hall and the elevator. There was no one about they could see, so they returned to the instruction room.

"Okay. Let's get Doe out here and explain the facts of life to her. She can teach us to use the machinery," Z said, as he opened her door.

There was no one there.

"ET? Joe? Where did she go?"

"She did not come out from her room, Z. We would not have allowed her to leave. I thought she was still there. Is there another door? Did she leave by another door? Was there a symbol for another room beyond her cubicle? She could not have left here. Joe and I have wands. We would have stopped her."

Z was standing in the cubicle. He noticed a sharp odor.

"Oh, my god! Ozone! Is there a panel in here?"

He checked the wall, and found a disposal panel by the door. He opened it to a sharp increase in the smell.

"It's opposite the one out there. Will someone please open the disposal panel?"

ET made some signs and pointed to the panel out there. Ape put his ring against the light and the panel opened. He was looking straight across at Z.

"There's an entrance to the panel on either side of the wall," Z said, as he closed the panel. "I several times made sarcastic remarks that the Peetoos were useless and that she was useless, too, because she served useless masters. She often said useless things were eliminated.

"I said it to try to shock her into showing some kind of emotion. I never thought it worked, but must have been wrong.

"Boy, was I wrong! When I said we were going to eliminate the Pweetoos aboard this ship, she must have thought I meant her, too. She beat us to it. Now I'll have *that* to live with!"

"No, no, Z. You did no wrong. It is not your fault if she cannot live without the Pweetoos. She served them, so she shares their evil. She was worse. The Pweetoos know no other way, but she did. She served them because she wanted to serve them. She was evil. That is no fault of ours. I will not take a guilt that is not mine, and you should not take one that is not yours. You have done no wrong. She was evil. Even Thing would not let her too close. Even Thing knows she was evil. There is no guilt. Do not seek what is not there."

Z put a hand on ET's shoulder.

"Thanks," he said. "In any case, what's done is done. We can't go back and change it one whit!"

Z sat on a bench and Joe sat close to him. Thing reached a tentacle to wrap lightly around his neck. ET sat on a close bench, while Ape prowled around the room, watching the door.

It had to be done very quickly if it was to be done at all, but this left him in a bad spot. He didn't yet know how to pilot the ship, and it was more than half bluff when he said he could use the machines to learn how.

He could probably learn anything he wanted from those machines – that, assuming there was no saturation point – except how to use the machines. That was a point he had studiously avoided, until now, but it was one that must be faced. He hoped there were written instructions.

That was one hell of a lot of "maybe" and "if" to worry about. He'd never really believed they could take over the ship. Not deep down. He'd hoped, basically, to get into a position to bargain for getting them home.

Had they gone too far?

Z couldn't doubt the only way anyone was going home was if they did it themselves. It was far past the point of threats or bargaining. The guards were dead and Doe was dead. The pilot down there couldn't be made to do anything.

He couldn't let the others see he was sick with fear and worry. He spent half his life going off half-cocked, in one way or another, but he could always talk his way out of it.

On Earth. With Earthlings! Talk had no value, whatever, out here. The best time to think about all this was before they killed the first guard. It was too late at that moment to ever try to retreat.

Had he gotten these trusting people into a worse mess than they would have been in anyhow?

No. Doe said they would have been eliminated. Whatever they had lost, they did still have life. He just wasn't sure they had hope.

Only one way to go. Forward.

He sighed, squared his shoulders, and demanded of his mind that it work!

"Now, we've really got to come up with some plan to mop up this deal," Z said. "I don't think there's much danger from what's left of them now. They're 'way too specialized to cause much trouble.

He signaled for them all to come to the main console. He studied the controls for a few minutes, then said, "I'm in a dilemma. How do we handle this? Do we lock the rest of the Pweetoos in one of the cells? Do we kill them all? Do we drop them off on some planet?

"ET, we have to all vote on this. I just can't take anymore responsibility for this onto myself. I've screwed up enough, already. You explain to Ape and Joe, and we'll vote on whatever options we have."

"It will not work, Z. Ape will do what he thinks you want and Joe will follow him to please you. It is still only your decision. Ape only seeks your approval. You have approved killing the Pweetoos and you will find that is his vote, as it is mine. It is started, so must be finished. There are many things, once started, where the road is not seen ahead, but those paths have fences, so a person may not turn to the side. You must go forward. That is a story from my world. It is very true, Z. The dead can never live again, and that means we must go ahead. It is a thing already decided. Every time we do something we will cause something else to have to be done. It is the way of all things, forever. It is decided. We may lose or we may win, but we may *not* stop! I am sorry that I talk so much."

"I guess that's true enough. Ape is pretty bloodthirsty, and will enjoy the kill," Z said resignedly. "We're probably stuck without a choice, anyway. We could never trust them."

"No! That is not true, Z. Ape is not bloodthirsty. Ape is gentle. He does not wish to kill. That is something you have taught him. He is gentle."

"No! You can't lay that on me!" Z cried. "You've seen how Ape reacts to killing them! He grins enough to split his face open!"

"No, Z. You know that is not true. Ape wishes to please you."

"Don't do this to me, ET," Z begged.

"You know it is true. Everything Ape does, he does for you. He looks to you and you grin. It is his sign that he has done well. It is a thing you have taught to him. You approve. It is your approval if you grin. He grins to seek approval, you grin to show it and he grins to show he likes the approval. Not the killing. It is not because he enjoys it. He knows it must be, so he does it. It is for all of us, and he knows he is much stronger. He knows you can think best. Ape looks ferocious, but how a person looks means nothing. Ape is very gentle."

"Damn it, ET...."

"It is not his fault he is here and it is not anyone's fault we are here except the Pweetoos. If we do not kill them, they will kill us. It is that simple. Ape knows that, you know that, I know that, Joe knows that and, I believe, Thing knows that."

"ET ... I suppose I know it."

"You want to be guilty, Z. I do not understand why you want to be so guilty. All the things you say you are sorry for are things that must be. Please do not take guilt for things you cannot control. Do not make yourself guilty when you are not. It is true. You do that."

Z stared at the floor. "I guess I know it, ET. I just can't handle the extra pressure. I don't want to lower myself to the Pweetoos' level. I want to be more than that!"

He shook his head and buried his face in his hands. "Well, I guess we couldn't ever make them understand, anyway."

ET replied, "I can talk to them very well. We have all been practicing. We have a lot of hand signs. We had time while we waited. We have learned..." They heard the door to the next room click and buzz. Z jumped to his feet and called, "Ready!"

Ape and Joe rushed to their positions by the door. Thing sprang to Ape's shoulder.

Zeekou came into the room. It looked around and went to the console, where it set the machine to translate.

"What is the meaning of this?" it demanded.

Z answered, "We've taken over the ship. We're going back home."

Zeekou pushed switch nine and depressed it. It held it down for fifteen seconds.

"All the guards will come. You will all be eliminated. We will not tolerate this defiance! Prepare to die! No one defies the Pweetoo!"

"The guards are all dead," Z retorted. "You'll do as you're told or you'll join them. We're out of patience with you and your threats. *We* are the ones who won't tolerate anymore from *you*!"

Zeekou pushed another of the switches. "I think not!"

A moment later, Eerf marched into the room. It spoke with Zeekou for a minute in the high-pitched whine, then picked up the microphone, and looked at Z. "You will all return to your cell! Now!"

Z stared him in the eyes.

"You *dare* to defy *me*?! I am a second caste high! I will order the elimination of your entire species! *Go*! I order it! Immediately!"

"How will you order the elimination of our species?" Z asked. "You'll be dead!"

"It makes no difference. The ship has recorded where each of you came from. My termination means nothing."

"But *we* have the ship!" Z sneered.

"You cannot use the ship. You are not bred to pilot. It is hopeless," Eerf said, haughtily. "Go to your cell! Now!"

"We aren't insects!" Z shouted. "We can use the ship!"

"Wait, Z!" ET cried. "Stop!"

He turned to Eerf. "Pweetoo, it may be true that we cannot use the ship. The female Immin here thought we may be able to learn from the machine. She felt we could use the wands to force her to teach us how to use the machines. She was told of our plan to kill your brood mother in revenge for you kidnapping us and killing our friend, Bear. She was loyal to you. She went into the disposal to thwart us in our plan, but that does not matter. We can use *you* to learn where to find the brood mother. We can put Ape and Joe on the machine and learn how to extract the information from your minds. You cannot stop us. We will use the information from your minds to find and kill your brood mother."

Eerf turned back toward Zeekou and made a sharp command. Zeekou didn't react.

"We can make the ship do what we say," ET continued. "It is not our species that will be eliminated, it is yours. We will kill the brood mother and you will all die. That will be the end of the evil Pweetoos. We know this is true. There is but one brood mother on one world. If she dies, you cannot further breed, so the whole world will die. We will take where the world is from your minds. You cannot stop us."

ET looked at Z, then back to Eerf. "You will go now into the room behind this one while we experiment on Joe and Ape with the machine. Unplug your wands. You will not be able to escape the room without them. It is decided. Do not resist us. It is you who are without hope. Doe thought she could save your world by killing herself. That is not true. We have you and we have the machine and the ship. You are doomed. You are without hope, and so is your brood mother!"

He reached up to unplug Zeekou's wand from the power pack and looked to Eerf, who unplugged its own and handed it to him. ET handed the wands to Joe and opened the door to Doe's cubicle. Eerf and Zeekou went inside and he closed the door.

"What the hell was that all about, ET?" Z asked.

"It is done, Z," ET replied.

"What's done?"

"Oh, Z. I have a plan where we don't have to kill all the Pweetoos. They will kill themselves. I could not discuss it with you, because there was no time. I thought of it from the female, Doe. She told you about the brood mothers. The brood mother is the all. They must kill themselves to save the brood mother. Look!"

He pointed to the light beside the disposal wall panel. One flickered.

"They do not think we can find the brood mother if they are dead. They know the machine can take anything that is in their minds. They do not question that we would use Ape and Joe to learn how to use those machines, because they would use any of their own kind. They are too limited and they feel nothing for anything. They cannot see we would never use any of us in an experiment. Zeekou would use any under him and Eerf would do the same, even using Zeekou. They must save the mother. If that means they die, they will do it. Look."

The light flickered again.

"Let us now open the door. They will be no more. They did what I told them Doe did. They have gone into the disposal. They must stop danger to the brood mother, and that is a way. The brood mother is now safe."

They went into Doe's cubicle to find it empty, but smelling sharply of ozone.

"I'll be damned!" Z exclaimed. "ET, you make me feel like a retarded monkey. You can come up with a plan like that on the spur of the moment while all I could think of was to bash their heads against the wall!"

He waved Ape and Joe to the console. Thing transferred from Ape to Z.

"We've got to search the ship. We have to get rid of the rest of the Pweetoos. We probably can't hope to talk all of them into suiciding, because the translator's in here. It's a mop-up operation now."

"I do not understand, Z. Why must we mop? The ship seems to clean itself. There in no blood or anything, even where there were things."

"Damn it all, ET! It's just an idiom! 'Mop up' means to rid ourselves of whoever's left! Sheesh!"

"Please do not use these idioms, Z."

"The next problem's the pilot, so let's get at it," Z said, thoroughly expecting ET to ask him what they were to get at and why, but ET just made a small grin and shook his head, then signaled for the others to come.

Z led them to the elevator. It was crowded, and Thing went to Ape's shoulder, as there was more room there than on any of the rest of them. Z took them to the observation dome, first. He explained to ET that they would have to search the entire ship and they could hold the elevator at whatever floor they wished by jamming the door. No one could get past them in the pilot's dome.

The dome disturbed Joe and ET a bit, but they stayed close to the others and were soon over it. They became fascinated with the red star, so Z explained what he was doing while they looked.

"You see, ET, we now know you and Joe are nervous in the domes. It's better to know now than if we have to act in the other one."

They went back into the elevator, and Z took them to the opposite dome. He didn't warn them of the gravity reversal and didn't revolve the elevator. He enjoyed the surprised look on Ape's face. Thing wasn't impressed, though it was never much impressed by anything. Joe enjoyed it and made a giggling laugh. ET asked, "How do they do that?"

Z laughed, and said, "Artificial gravity" as he revolved the elevator. Ape grabbed for the side when the elevator began to revolve, then looked sheepish when he didn't fall. He made a sound between a growl and a chuckle. Z saw the excited look on his face and surmised it was his laugh.

The pilot was still the only occupant of the dome. Z walked over and tapped the helmet. The Pweetoo looked at him, pressed the switch for nine, saw the others, and held it down.

"The guards ain't a-comin'," Z drawled. "They's all done

daid!"

The Pweetoo turned back toward the console and ignored him, though he tapped the helmet harder.

Ape came over and tapped the helmet hard enough to rock the Pweetoo. It refused to look up.

Ape grasped the helmet on either side and yanked it off the pilot's head. A piece of the head came away with it. The helmet was glued on. Ape was staring wide-eyed at the dripping helmet. He looked nervously at Z.

"You look like a whipped dog, Ape," Z said. "It's okay. You just don't know your own strength. We would've had to kill it, anyhow."

Ape looked from Z to ET and back again, getting even more agitated.

"Ape, it's okay ... oh, I get it!"

He grinned widely at Ape, who looked relieved, and held the helmet out to him. Z took it, and signed for Ape to dump the body into the ever-present disposal unit, while he scraped the mess out of the helmet. He may have to wear the thing! It was as much as certain someone would!

"Now we have to search the rest of the ship," Z said. He waved them back to the elevator.

They went to the main floor, where Z signaled for Joe and ET to go to opposite positions in the hallway. With Ape and Z before door one, ET by door eight, and Joe before door four, they could see the entire hall at all times.

Ape and Z started at room one and would search a room, then all would move one room clockwise until they were back to room one and all had been searched.

Thing moved back to Joe. It occurred to Z that Thing was always riding on someone, but you were never really conscious of it. He supposed it would have as much trouble moving about the smooth floors as the Pweetoos did. Tentacles weren't exactly designed for that.

Z was careful to have Ape on one side of the door and

him on the other when they opened them.

Room one: dot: cargo room. Door opened immediately. All the others had the ten to fifteen second delay. Power sphere of the type he'd studied. Miscellaneous machinery and ... other stuff.

Both green and orange lights under the symbol. File that. There was a reason for everything, here.

Room two: line: instruction room: Doe's cubicle.

Room three: triangle: interrogation room. Cubicle.

Room four: square: interrogation room. Cubicle.

Room five: triangle/line: cell.

Room six: 2 triangles: Their cell.

Room seven: square/triangle: equipment. Cubicle.

Room eight: 2 squares: wouldn't open. A sign flashing in green under the symbol as soon as it was struck said the alien atmosphere inside was methane, ammonia, nitrogen, hydrogen and sulfur dioxide. Alien atmosphere. Green means danger in Maitan code.

Room nine: square/triangle/line: bunkroom.

Room ten: square/2 triangles: food prep. Equipment.

Z met the others in front of room one. "There's no one else here, at all! I can't understand where ... well, it looks like we're going home!

"We have to take our time. We have to study the ship and how it works. We need rest.

"We've won! Let's hope the victory doesn't mean we're stuck here to starve or something!"

It had gone so much better than he could possibly have dreamed. Only Bear was gone from the original group, and that was a thing that was never under his control. The ship was searched, and there was simply no way anyone could be on it they didn't know about.

The problem was, he didn't know how to fly the ship. He didn't want to say anything to scare the others just yet, but something Eerf said had chilled him, and he wasn't in the least over that fear. It had, as a matter of fact, grown. That was why he didn't want to rush into anything so far as tinkering with the ship was concerned.

The Pweetoos didn't lie. They weren't capable of it.

Eerf said the ship knew where each of them came from and that the Pweetoos would "eliminate" their entire species from existence. If he made a mistake the threat could become reality. He had no way to know just how much the ship was programmed to do on its own. His study session about the power spheres made him suspect it could do a great deal more than give him any feeling of safety or control. He knew the power storage spheres were composed of special materials and that there was some kind of force field – he could build one, given the parts, but he didn't have any idea how it worked – in the physical sphere that, quite literally, held pure energy between the separate dimensional planes.

The "N" plane is the one we're all familiar with, the one in which we exist. The other was a "TTH" plane. The math was far beyond his ability to understand.

His worry there was that the ship held constant control over those two planes when the spheres were in use. That meant that the ship was capable of independent decision-making!

Z doubted the Pweetoos knew much about the potential of the complex ship. They simply copied another one without beginning to understand – like he could build a sphere that would work perfectly, but he didn't have clue one as to how those violent force fields could exist in two universes at once.

What if he couldn't pilot the ship? What if none of them could? What if he couldn't find a way to stop the ship from wiping their races out?

One thing was certain. He knew those power spheres inside and out and he knew they contained energies far beyond his puny imaginings. He also knew how he could cause them to release all their energy at once, making a multimegaton hydrogen bomb look like a fourth of July sparkler.

He had no doubt a quick meeting would have all these beings aboard the ship agreeing to die to save their worlds. This ship and all aboard would be expanding gases in a millisecond.

It mustn't come to that. It was still a ship, only a machine, and it still could and would be controlled. There were exact instructions, written instructions, for all kinds of things, so he was sure they could find the manual for the teaching machines.

How he hated the idea of using the teaching machine again! The headache from the last time was still there!

Bite the bullet and all that crap. If he had to, he had to.

He lay back in the pilot's chair and fiddled with the dials on its side. It was quite comfortable, but it could be made better.

Adversity did strange things to people. Here he was in a spaceship, God knew where, with four very different kinds of creatures. One, he couldn't begin to classify and three who seemed to be mammals.

Doe was a mammal.

Did that mean that mammals were the only intelligent life in the universe?

The Pweetoos weren't mammals, but were they really what you could call intelligent?

Well, yes. Collectively, they had to be. Individually, it didn't matter. The individual cells in the brain are stupid. It's the combination that works.

Where did he read that theory? Omni? Discover? The Sciences? Somewhere. Social insects aren't true individuals. The colony or hive was the individual.

Off on tangents. Maybe that would do him good.

ET had said that Doe, the Immin woman, was evil. He had an undeniable, simplistic logic to back what he said. She had a choice, and had chosen to aid the Pweetoos. Even he knew, from his reactions to her, that she was hiding her real self. He had sensed her arrogance and deviousness.

The Pweetoos weren't evil, by ET's definition. They were neutral – because they had no choice.

ET constantly surprised him with insights lightyears past his apparent intelligence.

Don't think in terms of lightyears. That's 'way too close to home in this situation!

Joe was definitely lacking in the intelligence area, and Z still felt the little guy had spent his entire lifetime being kicked around. At first, Joe had followed him, and probably always would, but he was turning to Ape, now. Z was glad of that. He wasn't the adored-hero type. It just embarrassed him. He had often seen Joe sitting close to Ape and watching him in rapt adoration.

Ape was strength, to Joe. Ape would never be kicked around, because he was too strong. Hadn't he even grinned and laughed at the wand?

Ape. His Wooky.

Ape was more intelligent than he showed. Probably more

than Z, so far as natural intelligence went. Book learning wasn't intelligence. Solving problems was.

Ape also had a great sense of humor. Z could feel that.

Thing, curled in his lap right now, was an enigma.

Maybe ET was right. Maybe it was highly intelligent, but different. It had certainly come through when the chips were down! Big time!

There was something that made you feel good when Thing was riding around on you. Something calming.

What a group! This was even further out than those stupid supermarket tabloids!

The ship was the real problem, now. He must find a way to pilot this thing and get them out of here! It was too much to ask that it would be simple.

The times he had put the helmet on, he found that the ship could almost take over his mind, and that scared him. It made him remember ET saying they could get anything they wanted from Eerf's mind to use to kill the brood mother. The Pweetoos had never doubted a word of that! They knew it was true!

So. How could he put that headgear on and allow the ship to get into his mind? How could he pilot the thing if he didn't?

He had to get the manual and learn what was in store from the helmet and how to pilot the ship – the ship that scared hell out of him!

Thing rolled around a bit, then wrapped a tentacle around his neck, but it wasn't in the way.

The ship was just a ship, and was their friend, so there was no need to fear it.

Where the hell did *that* come from?!

Well, he was projecting too much into the ship. It wasn't some brooding monster hovering about, ready to consume them. The danger was the Pweetoos. The thing he wasn't sure he could handle was the fact they would be traveling many times the speed of light.

Silly. The problem was navigation.

When he put the helmet on, it always first called for data coordinates and opened – something. Something he was then supposed to do with the dials and switches on the main console. Colored buttons and levers. Twelve numbers and four letters. Exact route markers. Pulsar triangulation. It would all make sense when he found the manual. He didn't learn to read without a reader, he didn't learn arithmetic without his tables, and he wouldn't learn to pilot this ship without the manual.

Part two

Retribution

Learning

It was pure luck. It had to be.

Z sat on the bench in front of the main console, trying to make some kind of sense of the dials and switches. He hadn't found the first manual about the machines, but had found the settings for the various courses. He still didn't know how to start the machine.

Z had to sit close to the console, so Thing, who was riding on him at the time, climbed onto the screen above the console, which Z had learned was called a central consolidated holovid comstation. He was frustrated and was studying the overly-complicated settings, and had programed to receive the basic instruction on piloting the ship, when Thing slipped. Z had the helmet on, so couldn't catch it. He only saw it when it caught his peripheral vision. It grabbed outward as it fell to the bench and wrapped a tentacle around a small lever on the side of the console, pulling it down as it fell.

Z blacked out. When he awakened, he again had the violent headache – and he knew how to pilot the ship! Thing had hit the proper lever to engage the program he had set, the program was ready to go!

He also knew how to use the machines, now. That seemed more than strange, as it was *not* part of the piloting program.

Well, he had programmed in a few things on guesses, and he had always been lucky, that way.

He spent the next few days using the teaching machine to learn all that was available about the ship. He could set it at a lower rate, The headaches were still intense, but much more bearable. The things he'd learned about the power spheres made it far easier, because it was basic to most of the other sciences aboard the ship.

He had been wise not to enter the engine room, though the danger wasn't acute unless the ship was in another mode, or dimensional planal construct, as it was called. The power sphere was used to run the internal parts of the ship, only, and to engage the ID drive. The drive drew directly from dimensional stress when in "motion." Lower than lightspeed drive was accomplished through hydrogen diffusion, which had to do with collecting the ubiquitous hydrogen atoms in space and fusing them. That was the dangerous part in the engine room, as it produced intense but shortlived radiation.

Atmospheric drive was handled solely by the power sphere. It worked through an odd sort of capacitance/repulsion process.

That was not really what happened, but it was the way he interpreted the data. So long as he could use it well, what difference did the terminology make?

He learned that motion, as he knew it, was possible in a few of the "planes" the ship could use. Those were in the TTH designations. In others, the fact the omniverse is a point meant one could enter those "planes" at an angle that would "shift base perspective" from the energy balance restoration, which allowed the ship to leave the "plane" at a projected location, dropping into "N" space lightyears from where the ship entered the "plane" here.

See?

He didn't, really. Maybe that was Einstein's wormholes.

The dimensional "planes" were actually other universes that make up the omniverse and dimensions weren't what Z had been taught. Length, width, and height were all parts of the dimension called "structure." The "angles" were stressed quite differently, in other "planes." Time/ Motion (The same thing, in a way) is the basic dimension and the only reality (!). The rest of it is perception. It must add up to zero to exist at all.

That is, the omniverse. It must always remain in absolute balance. The only true equation in the structural omniverse is $N = -N$.

In other words distance in the N plane does not translate as distance in other planes. Time is variable in a given plane, but constant in a specific one – though the perception of time may vary, due mostly to inertial effects.

Distance is length. Find a plane where length is a closer angle or where there *is* no distance or where length is a specific fraction of the N plane definition and one may be able.... He could use it. That was what mattered. The *ship* did all the figuring of planes.

The various astronomical bodies, such as stars, in planes with structural dimensions ... caused turbulence, which must be avoided. The pilot's job, basically, was to avoid the turbulences. The ship detected the turbulence, the pilot went around it. That was his function.

Why didn't some kind of automatic circuit do that?

Return to N plane in such a body and reverse the charge in the moder, which means you are suddenly antimatter in the same space as matter.

Whooo! Convert the *entire mass* to energy!?! A whole *star*!?! In *both* Planes?!?

There were antimatter planes. One for each matter plane. Force fields protected the ship in those planes, but many ships didn't have such shields, thus couldn't use those planes.

I guess *not*!

Some planes were of pure energy. Some lacked certain other subdimensions. Some had more subdimensions. Trips could only be figured inside the galactic area, as physics changed outside the gravity fields. Ships had left for other galaxies, but none had ever been heard of again. They were "thrown" through null space and could be lost in other universes or might simply be lost "jumping" from galaxy to galaxy with no way to know where they were.

Those were only theories. They might have actually gotten somewhere. Some had been going for a hundred thousand years. It wasn't entirely impossible one or more of those ships would one day wander back home.

Unless the dimensions were "stretched" to where they lost all substance and became part of the black matter.

Physics might be different in other galaxies. They might be the same everywhere. From what he understood, they would be the same in each galaxy, but different in a comparative sense – if the observer were in a position outside either.

Why not just say it wasn't safe to try to leave the galaxy, and there certainly wasn't any reason to, seeing as only about a hundredth of a percent of this one had been explored in the past hundred thousand years!

The Pweetoos depended on slowly moving outward, considering that interstellar navigation wasn't nearly so easy as was once predicted. Once a star system was physically visited, the ships could "remember" how to get there and back. They moved like an expanding balloon, slowly doing a total telescopic search, then going about thirty lightyears, maximum, in about two hundred years. The Maitans had gone slowly, but at a faster rate.

All very interesting, but what Z learned was that he was the only one who could hope to pilot the ship. The pilot must be able to read Maitan quickly and accurately. Any hesitation could mean disaster. Joe and Ape couldn't speak *or* read and ET couldn't read.

The plus was, the ship could return automatically anywhere it had ever been, part of which was their own home worlds. The course was on automatic plot. Drift meant a very small distance variation in calculations, but what was a mere few billion plus or minus kilometers to such a ship?

They were no longer in a hurry, now that they were safe, and the headaches must have time to wear away. They would cause delays in reactions in piloting, which could be disastrous. The food was still delivered automatically to their original panels, so there was no problem, there.

Z wanted to learn as much as he possibly could before attempting to pilot the ship, so he studied the computers and how to use them. He studied the way the coils twisted space around itself, actually placing the ship inside its own moder. He studied the theory behind the wands and why changing the resistance, all the buttons did, changed the character of the photonic energy they used.

Not until then did he feel he would ever be able to control the ship's computers well enough to withdraw from any other dangerous situation.

When he tried to use the main computers, he sometimes got strange reactions. The computer seemed to be in a state of a strange kind of shock, possibly from the violent loss of its Pweetoo pilot. After all, it was wearing the helmet when it died.

The machine sometimes even seemed to be trying to start a personal conversation. In a way, Z wanted to get chatty with the machine, but he was afraid it could use the openness to get into his mind, and he dare not lose control.

ET spent much of his time exploring the amazing ship, and learned a great amount about where everything was. Joe always went with him and Ape was usually there, too, with Thing on his shoulder. Thing spent its time hanging on them all.

Z turned to communications, and learned each ship had a built-in beacon that kept its location noted at all times in master computers on all the Pweetoo-controlled planets to be colonized by the particular brood mother's offspring that owned it. Should any beacon cease transmitting, a rescue ship was immediately dispatched to its last known location. The only thing that could stop beacon transmission was a disaster to the ship – or so the Pweetoos reasoned.

Z discussed this with ET. That meant the Pweetoos could trace them back to their home planets, even though they had the ship. That gave validity to the threat Eerf made. The ship very well could, absolutely and positively, return to each of their home planets – and so could any other Pweetoo ship used by the brood mother who owned this one.

It was good Z had waited. It would give them time to do something about their beacon. As long as it was operating, it was literally impossible to hide anywhere in the area of the Pweetoo Empire.

There were no other long-distance communications, as the sending sets were reasonably simple in design and theory, but they consumed truly prodigious amounts of energy. The receivers were tremendously complex. The basic drain on the power sphere was the beacon sending circuits.

Z called the group together in the instruction room, room two.

"We've got one hell of a problem, guys," he lectured. "The ship transmitted where we came from and we can't do anything about it. I'm not sure what we can do, as I don't know how the Pweetoos will react to the loss of the ship. We have to know if they'll retaliate against our home planets.

"I'm going to study the Pweetoos' history, though I really didn't want to get into that. It may give me a clue as to how they'll act."

He looked around the group.

"ET, please explain what's happening to the others. We've talked about a lot of this. I'm going back on the machine to get myself another headache."

"All right, Z, but can't we disconnect the transmitting machine so the Pweetoos will not know where to find us? I do not know how these things work. Can we turn the power off? You say the beacon takes most of the power of the energy sphere. Can't we take the wires off? Would that stop the beacon?"

"I plan to disconnect it, ET, but I'll have to wait until we're about to move. They'll send a ship to where we were when it stopped transmitting. We don't know if there's any Pweetoo ship nearby, so we don't know how long we have to get away."

Z went to the console, set the machine for the Pweetoo history and put the headset on. He was there for about two hours. When he finished, he took the helmet off and sat it on the bench. He looked like he'd aged about ten years. He put his face in his hands and hunched over. Thing came to climb into his lap and peer intently into his eyes. It put the tentacle tip against the side of his face and stroked him. He absentmindedly stroked the little animal. Joe was kneeling to one side and kept grabbing at his free hand. ET was to the other side.

"Oh, Z! Z! What is the matter, Z? Please, Z, whatever has happened? I am afraid, again! You are ill! Please, please, Z, what is the matter? Please speak!"

Z shook himself dully and looked up. "Oh, my god, guys!" he wailed. "I can't believe it! I can't believe what I've just seen!

"Using the machine is like seeing their history through the eyes of a high caste Pweetoo.

"God! The things they've done! They feel absolutely no emotion. None whatever. That's why they didn't retaliate when I yanked one into the hall wall or when Ape kicked one across the room.

"They've completely destroyed some fine civilizations. I mean, destroyed! Killed off the entire race!

"They have weapons that will split a planet open. They have one that will cause a sun to nova and destroy more than one planet at a time.

"Oh, my god! And just because some brood mother feels she's threatened or because she says they're useless to her! I can't believe it!

"The units, such as those we killed on this ship, only live from nine to ten, uh, time periods, as adults. A time period is about eight or nine Earth months. They live a bit more than six Earth years as adults. Eerf was almost that old, so didn't mind dying. Its only purpose, like any of them, was to serve the brood mother.

"If the brood mother dies, the whole colony will die out in less than ten years. There are only a few brood mothers, each on an individual planet. They're insects of a single-structured societal type. Social insects. Rigid evolution that won't allow more than one brood mother on a given world. They commit truly unbelievable atrocities against their own kind, as well as against others. They have brood wars. The losers become slaves to the winners. Members of one brood can't even approach the planet of another brood. Where the brood worlds are is kept secret, except from the brood there.

"We've defied them by taking this ship. They'll go to any length for revenge. They'll very definitely destroy our home planets unless *we* stop them!

"It's not revenge, as we know it. There's neither anger nor hatred. It's just a psychological imperative. The logic is that we've destroyed the Pweetoos here, so are an unspecified danger to the brood mother; therefore, we must be eliminated. If we can do it, others of our races can do it. They must be eliminated. They are best eliminated by destroying the very worlds they inhabit."

He shook his head and stood. "We must stop them!"

ET picked up the headgear. "I must see, Z. Please set the machine."

"No, ET. You can't ... I guess you have to, don't you?"

"Yes, Z. It is not a thing I wish, it is a thing that must be. I do not like the idea that one being must harm another. I run away from that. I cannot run away if my home and my people are threatened. I wish to run, but I will not. Please set the machine, Z."

Z's shoulders drooped as he went to the console like a sleepwalker. He set the machine, and they all sat in silence until ET was through. He sadly removed the headgear, with tears flowing.

"Oh, Z! Oh, Ape! Oh, Joe! Thing! It is terrible! They are a disease! It is horrible! They are sickness! I am sick! Come to me, Thing. I need you. Oh, Z! This is beyond what I had thought. They are terrible! I do not care that I have killed them. They have no spirits, so it is not as though they are people. They are purely sickness. They are not people. How can the Immins serve them? They are disease!"

He held out his hand, and Thing went to him to wrap the tentacles around him. Joe sat close against him and Ape went to take his chin into an enormous hand and look deeply into his eyes.

Ape picked up the helmet and pointed to the console. Z shrugged and set the controls. ET breathed a heavy sigh and hugged Thing to him.

"I'm really a bit worried about Ape seeing that history," Z warned. "Can you picture him running amok?"

"I think I know what you mean. I think it will be all right. I am more worried for when Joe sees it. He is so afraid. I worry. Ape is very strong and will not be harmed.

Joe is not strong. I worry."

"I am *not* putting Joe on that machine! That's final!" Z retorted.

"No, Z. You do not have the right to refuse. He will have to see. He has a home and he must know. We are all in this. It is not a thing that any have rights about. It is a duty we must all face."

"I know you're right. I just don't want to do it. It could ruin his mind, ET!" Z replied, dejectedly.

"I know. I'm afraid for him, also. It must be."

They looked over to see little Joe, who was sitting tightly against Ape and watching his face intently.

"Do not worry for Ape, Z. He is strong and he is good. He will not harm any of us. I am not afraid of Ape. He will handle this well."

"Im not worried about what Ape will do to us, I'm worried about what this will do to Ape," Z responded.

They waited, and Ape eventually took the helmet off. He had a hunted look. Ape ruffled the top of Joe's head and patted Thing, who had joined Joe a few minutes before, then stood and went out of the room. Z started after him, but ET stopped him.

"No, Z. Let him be alone. It is his nature. He must work it out for himself. It is his way."

Joe inspected the helmet carefully and put it on. He was trembling violently. He sat in a crouch and waited. Thing had wrapped him in the tentacles and waited with him.

"He knows you must. There is no reason to wait. Do it now, Z," ET said, quietly.

Z set the machine and shuddered as he saw Joe stiffen. He laid close on the bench beside Joe and tried to doze to relieve the headache. After a time, ET said, "Z," and pointed to Joe. Z went to take the helmet off. Joe cowered down on the bench and looked terrified. ET went to put an arm around him and sat close, rocking him, with Thing's tentacles around both of them.

Thing sidled along the bench to the helmet. It studied the gear and put it on its head.

"No, Thing," Z said, and lifted the helmet, but Thing had tentacles around the helmet and was lifted with it. It held the headgear tightly to its head, and wouldn't let go.

"It has a right, too, Z. It has a home. Maybe the machine will not reach its mind. It can die. It nearly did, helping us. It has a home and people who can die there. It has the right."

Z drooped his shoulders. He set the machine.

Ape came in and saw Thing on the machine. He spun around to face Z with pure fury on his face. For the first time in all this, Z feared for his life.

"No, Ape!" came from ET. "Come here."

He waved for Ape to come to him. Ape stood uncertainly for a second, then went to ET, who had a silent argument with him in sign language. Ape relented when ET picked the helmet up to have Thing still holding it on with the two upper tentacles. Ape looked sheepishly at Z, who shrugged and grinned a grim grin.

When the machine stopped, a much shorter time with Thing, it went to Ape's shoulder and reached a tentacle out to Z. That more than anything convinced Ape it was Thing's choice to go onto the machine. Joe and ET came over to be wrapped in tentacles.

"All for one and one for all," Z quoted.

"Yes, that is true. We must all stay together. We must stop them from ever happening again. They are a disease that must be cured. We must make a solid plan. How can we ever destroy the Pweetoos? It is not possible!"

"I've got an idea," Z offered. "We can use the spheres and wands to get the brood mothers. With them gone, the hive dies in a few years. They will have no organization without the brood mother.

"The only problem is finding where they are – and I think I know how if I can get that crazy computer to work!"

Z carefully restudied the power spheres Doe's program had earlier explained to him. The spheres were of a material that could exist in two planes at once by forming a force field in a matrix held on the inside of a hollow impervium vessel. It was necessarily spherical, as that was the shape of a force field.

The energy inside the sphere was more than that outside the sphere, so a small "leak" was supplied to allow the energy a path out. The energy was almost a photonic fluid, and the use system changed the fluid to whatever type of energy was needed through various resistance shunts. The smallest spheres held about as much energy as was released in a medium hydrogen bomb explosion. The largest spheres, such as connected on this ship, held more than four times that amount.

The energy could be easily transferred from one sphere to another, but the problem the Pweetoos saw was in the absolute capacity of a sphere. The spheres were already at the limits, lower and upper, that could be utilized. They didn't have the ability to see the spheres could be attached in series, thus allowing any amount to be stored. Their limited way of seeing things said, first, that they needed ten times the energy storage of even the largest spheres and, second, that the present spheres couldn't handle the excess. It would never occur to their logic system that one could simply use several spheres. They felt they needed more storage in one sphere.

The only use for such amounts of energy was weaponry.

He then spent two days, according to the clock they made that closely approximated Earth cycles, learning full usage of the ship's facilities, other than those in the pilot's dome. He was truly amazed at some of the things aboard. The equipment in room two alone would revolutionize science on Earth when he returned – and he was willing to make a semi-serious plan to return, now.

The holovid wasn't too greatly different from TV at home, except the photonic fluid energy was far more versatile than electricity could be. It was basically a three-D hologram driven by colored lasers.

The medboxes in room two could do almost anything he could imagine. They could virtually rebuild a body, if that body had ever been scanned. The monopolar devices made the microchip on Earth seem like a huge, unwieldy, inefficient, massive, slow, rusty broken-down old steam locomotive against a sleek rocket. This ship made rockets so obsolete the connection wasn't discernible.

The underlying theory of the fastcoms made it possible to communicate across the lightyears with no noticeable time lapse, though the energies needed would drain the biggest electric plants on Earth. Theories of interplanal dimensional cross-transference physics were completely beyond his meager abilities to begin to comprehend. The disposal units were called elementizers. They could separate anything dropped into them into individual atoms in only a few milliseconds. That was another use of photonic fluid.

He could dream!

One thing was certain: If he ever got home, he would cling to the memories of these friends he found here, and would keep his stupid damned mouth shut about it! The tabloids were wrong in their assertions that anyone would want to tell the world about an experience like this. It was his, and his alone, and he would never share it! Besides. He could picture what the people of Earth would do with the science. They would make the Pweetoos look downright saintly. Every little thing here could somehow be twisted and deformed into some kind of weapon.

Then he must concentrate on getting them out of here. His headaches were tolerable, he was rested, and he knew most of what he needed to know. He hoped.

He figured a way to communicate with other ships when they were in radio range. It was simple. The console in room two had a chart that gave the frequencies.

Most things were simple, if he took his time and looked to the computers for information.

His biggest problem had been what language to use here. Rather obviously, others would understand Maitan, but would these Pweetoos use Maitan in communicating among themselves?

He doubted it!

He set up a microphone to the radio and ran it through the translator machine. The machine would then send in Pweetoo and would translate the reply into Maitan. He had to be sure he didn't use any terms that wouldn't translate. *That* would certainly give it away!

At the end of the second day Joe came into the room, just as he was putting the equipment away. Thing was wrapped around his waist, as was its wont.

At first, Joe had retreated from the experience with the Pweetoo history, but seemed back to normal now. The companionship with Thing helped all of them in some vague undefinable way. Z suspected it was the unexpected warmth.

"I see you've recovered from the history lesson."

Thing put out a tentacle and drew them together.

"I get the message, little guy. It's good to have you back with us, Joe." He showed Joe some of the simpler things. Joe paid very close attention and Z thought about how hard the little fellow tried to be accepted as part of the group. Ape was patient with him and they were closer and closer. ET worked with all of them, and had a strong natural ability to communicate even complicated ideas to them. Even Thing seemed to understand the signs.

The next morning, Z called a general meeting. He used the PA system at the console in room two. They had staked out their own "rooms," and Z wasn't sure where they all were. He slept in the pilot's chair in the dome. It was the most comfortable spot he'd ever found, and was adjustable to any position he could dream up.

That was one of the first things he found from the teaching machine – how to adjust the chair. Apparently, the pilot went through some pretty trying times, so was pampered by such small comforts.

He knew Thing liked the cubicle in the rear of this room. It seemed to find Doe's bench a perfect place, when it wasn't wrapped around one of them. There was a teaching helmet in there, and Z sometimes wondered if Thing had been playing with it.

Oh, well. It wasn't likely the little guy could figure how to turn it on or select a program.

The others had their own spots. He had no idea where Joe or ET slept, but had found Ape's spot by accident. He went to the observation dome to study the red star, and had found Ape there, asleep. Ape had taken a couple of the larger thick mattresses from room nine to make himself a comfortable nest under the dome. Z respected the room as Ape's own private quarters. He didn't go there again.

When they were all assembled, he started the meeting.

"Okay, guys. It's time to get this show on the road. I'll expect ET to get the messages across to you. I know it may not be easy, but he tells me he's developed an excellent sign language with you.

"When I'm attached to the piloting comp I'll be as much as unconscious of my surroundings, when the ship's in transit. I'm connected directly to the computer circuits. ET's in charge at those times.

"As soon as I disconnect the locator beacon, we'll have to move. Fast!

"ET, it's vitally necessary you all understand that, once I'm moving the ship, I'm not to be disturbed for any reason. It could kill us all if I lose concentration for even one second.

"I know where to go to get new power spheres. They're recharged and left in various orbits for use by any of the Pweetoo ships. We'll pick up as many as we can carry and use them to bomb the brood mothers' dens. I can rig them to a wand with a timing device to make them explode whenever I want. It'll take a lot of math, but I think I can do it.

"After we pick up the spheres, I hope to be able to find the locations of the brood mothers from the computers.

"We all know just what the brood mothers are from the unpleasant history lesson. They're huge egg sacks with a small head. The mother head contains almost all the brains of the colony.

"They'll be underground, but our bombs have enough power to get them. When we find the planets they're on, it'll be easy to find the burrows. There will be enormous activity around the entrances as they bring food for thousands of larvae. That activity will locate them. This ship has excellent detection equipment, so we can find them from distant orbit.

"If anyone has any ideas or suggestions, at any time, I want to hear them. Fast. This is far too large an undertaking for our small group and one ship, but we simply have no choice. We're unlikely enough a group to have the fate of maybe millions of sentient beings dependent on us doing nothing less than a major miracle. I admit to being scared shitless!

"If there are no suggestions now I'll go to the dome to prepare to disconnect the beacon and make our first jump.

"Ape, don't go to the O dome when we're in transit. It may be safe and it may not. We can't take chances.

"I'll use the PA to tell you when we're leaving. It'll be less than one hour.

"Wish me luck?"

"You know we wish you luck, Z. Your luck is our luck and the luck of our homes. I have learned to talk with Ape and Joe very well with signs. I will tell them all you have said. We have the Pweetoo history to make us want to talk. I will have everyone ready."

He made a few fast signs. Ape signed back.

"Good luck, Z. We will die, if we must, but we will stop them from harming any others. It is time to stop them. We will do as you say. You will lead us."

Ape made a few signs, Joe added some, and ET made one.

"Since seeing the history, we do not feel we will ever be able to go home, but will die doing right. Our spirits will not wander alone. We will be together for all of time and more. We have been put here where no one wants to be. We will do what we must. You will tell us and we will follow you. We wish each of us good fortune in this, and we hope we can do enough that our homes are safe."

"*That* is one thing we have to all work toward," Z agreed. "It's time, as you said, they were stopped!"

"We will do nothing to distract you in any way when you are being pilot of the ship. We will not go into the pilot's dome unless you say it is safe. We will be very careful. You must be careful, too."

Z nodded and started out. Thing ran to him, so he picked it up and put it on his shoulder.

"I've missed you, too, little fellow. Come along, if you want."

Z went down to the pilot's dome, where he first opened the communications panel. He took a retainer off a lead connector and tied a piece of cord around it and through the catch ring on the door of the panel, then to the pilot's chair. He could sit in the chair and jump the ship, without getting up to pull the beacon lead apart. He wasn't sure how long it would take a rescue ship to arrive, and felt he might need every second, should he not be able to move the ship quickly enough. If it wouldn't go for him, all was lost.

They wouldn't know until they tried, and the computers did seem confused at times, but the data readings said the drive computers were separate from others and weren't affected.

No one knew how deeply and sincerely he wanted that to be true!

He went back to the drive console, where he quickly programmed the platform's coordinates into the main feed circuit. It was not unlike programming software for the Atari computers he worked with on Earth. This was the first time he'd worked with computers with his fingers crossed, though.

He went through the entire process in his mind as he read each and every dial and warning on the console. Even those that had nothing to do with flight. Nothing could be safely missed or misread.

After he was sure he had the routine rehearsed as well as possible, without any actual experience, he threw the com switch on the console to PA and announced, "We leave in exactly three minutes."

He set the timer on the panel to what he had learned was three minutes, and steeled himself for he knew not what.

He placed the headgear.

When the three minutes (that seemed like hours) had passed, he yanked the cord to disconnect the beacon and threw the drive headgear engagement switch, bringing his hand down hard to engage the flight plan. The only thing he remembered until the timer said they had been in flight for nine minutes sixteen seconds was a voice in his head that said, "Prepare for ID mode."

He was sure the flight had lasted more than ten minutes – by months! He was exhausted! When the ship is in flight, the pilot is directly a part of the computer. He sees two complete sets of controls on the console. One is what's happening and the other is what *should* be happening. It's the pilot's job to make them stay the same. Anyone who observes the pilot in action feels as if they're on a very different time scheme. The hands move so quickly they literally seem to blur. The pilot's reactions are so greatly enhanced he's quickly exhausted. He burns tremendous energy. It isn't recommended a pilot be in IDmode for more than thirty eight minutes in forty hours.

In short, the pilot does one week's work – very literally – in thirty eight minutes.

They re-entered "N-reality" a short distance from the orbit of a platform containing the energy spheres.

There was another ship there.

Z had hoped to find it empty of any other ship. A ship needed refueling only once in two or three years, so the odds against two vessels being at a platform at the same time were vanishingly small. He felt it might be a good time to try the radio setup he had planned, so he went to room two and the set. Once there, he set the translator for the necessary languages and frequency, picked up the microphone and said, "Will you be long in refueling? Z inquires."

He felt a surge of pure joy when, a moment later, an answer came: "We are partly through with the exchanging of the power pack. We will depart in approximately two dev. This is Poontaw responding, my Lord Z. Many szoondren!"

As he knew no more about what a szoondren was than

what a dev might be, he said, "Many...." and cut the transmission. He waited awhile by the com set, but received no further communications. Almost three hours later, the other ship simply flashed and was gone.

"Well, Thing!" Z said, petting the little animal, "At least we know a couple more things. When we leave in a flash, we *do* leave in a flash, and a dev is about an hour and a half."

He went to the console and turned on the PA. "I'm going on down to dock us to the platform. Be ready to get in the power spheres. They're safe to handle if you avoid hitting the part with the lights against anything. Don't touch the round piece between the lights. Be sure you all know that, ET.

"Where are you guys?"

A moment later ET came on the speaker. "We are in room one, the cargo hold. I felt we would have to go out to get the power spheres so I had us all come here to find the suits. We are all in suits and have checked how to open the big cargo door and how to get the air pumped out of the hold to save it. We are prepared to get the spheres, Z."

"You thought of a hell of a lot more than I did, ET," Z replied. "This is the first thought I'd given to how we'd get the spheres once we got here. I'm glad you're along, ET. We would've probably wasted hours, otherwise.

"I'm proud of you guys!"

"Thank you, Z. We had a lot of extra time while you were learning, so we sought out everything on the ship we felt we may need. It is best we know where things are and how they work. There are books with drawings, as well as drawings on many things here that tell how to use them. I need not know reading for drawings."

"Okay. I'll dock us in a minute," Z said, then went to the pilot's dome to bring the ship against the platform and drop magnetic grapples. He shut down the console and checked the drive readouts, then hitched Thing up to a more comfortable position as, he stood. It again occurred to him how easily they all took Thing for granted. They never really noticed it was there. It hadn't interfered in any way with his piloting of the ship, as he knew it wouldn't.

How did he know that?

Anyhow, he was very damned proud of that piloting, and he didn't care who knew it! First trip was a roaring success! Dead on target!

He went to the elevator, and was about to enter, when the cargo door opened. He stood to watch as a very large suited figure came out, along with a much smaller one. The smaller one clung very closely to the larger one for awhile, then became more sure of itself and would move away, checking the spheres. They made a lot of signs to each other. They seemed to be undecided.

The small figure turned to see Z was watching them and came close to the dome, raised its hands palm upward and shrugged. It was Joe, which surprised Z. He hadn't expected Joe to go out, judging from his reaction to the dome.

Z lifted his wand and pointed to the row of three buttons. He pointed to the spheres and to the orange button, then to the cargo door. He pointed to two other spheres and to the green button and shook his head "no."

He pointed to other spheres and the green button and shook his head "no," then to another and to the orange button, then to the cargo doors. He pointed to another of the spheres and then to the green button and shook his head "no."

Joe nodded and went back to Ape, where he began making signs and pointing to spheres. They went together to a sphere and looked around it to find the lights. Joe checked it over and waved for Ape to take it to the cargo hold.

Z went "up" to the instruction/medical room and turned the intercommunications PA on. He called for ET, but received no response. He checked the board, but could find nothing wrong.

He picked up the frequency chart and found the setting for the suits, set the radio and asked what was happening.

"Z, we have seven spheres. We have room for two more. I hope we are getting the proper ones. Joe signed it was you who told him how to select them. I hope we are correct."

"I'll be there in just a minute, as soon as I locate a portable transmitter," Z answered. He found hand-held transmitters on a shelf, and took one to set to the suits' frequency, then went to tap his wand against the symbol on the door to the hold. Nothing at all happened, so he checked the button and threw a spark. He had power.

He tried again. Nothing.

"What the hell!?" he snapped. "ET, where are you?"

"I am in the cargo hold, Z. I am helping to tie all these spheres so they will not roll."

"The damned door won't open!" Z cried.

"Of course not, Z. There is no air in here. We are open to space. The door has a thing so it won't open and let the air out of the ship."

"How can I be so damned *stupid*!?" Z cried. He looked at the symbol on the door, which was glowing green.

"Green. Empty. Danger. Cripes! I've should have known that without being told!"

He sat on the floor by the door with Thing in his lap and waited.

"ET, how much longer will it take? I really should program the ship to leave as quickly as we can. This may not be such a healthy place to be if that other Pweetoo ship was warned that any suspicious ship's missing."

"We are finished, Z. Please wait and check the spheres.

We must be sure they are the right ones. I am not sure. They all look alike."

"Just answer two questions, ET," Z replied. "Number one, how is Joe selecting the spheres?"

"He is finding the ones that are the same size as the ones you told him to take and they are all with the orange light glowing on the panel. We are tying them to magnetic anchor hooks."

"Now I *do* have another question!" Z exclaimed. "You're getting the correct spheres, but what do you mean about the size? I don't remember saying anything about size!"

There was a long pause before ET answered, "Joe says you pointed to the orange button on the wand and nodded yes, to take it to the cargo room. Then you pointed to three of the different-sized spheres and said no. You then pointed to another sphere the same size as the first, and said yes. He thinks you meant from the first that orange were good. You did not say yes to any green, so that was bad. You said yes to two same-size spheres and no to three different sizes. You said yes to only orange lights and no to all green lights. He is worried he misunderstood, and that we have done this work for nothing."

"No! He was absolutely right!" Z returned. "He was more right than I was! His logic was perfect. It'll be much easier to work with spheres that are all the same size – and they'll store easier, too! Tell him I'm proud of you guys and I'm especially proud of him!"

"We are almost ready to come in, then. You can check the spheres to see if they are the right ones. What was the other question, Z?"

"I just wondered how you sign who says what," Z said.

"You are one finger, held up, Z. I am two fingers. Thing is the thumb and Ape is the whole hand."

"I hope I'm not the middle finger," Z said. "I probably deserve to be!"

"What, Z?"

"Nothing. I was thinking out loud."

The door symbol flickered and went out and the door slid up. The group came out and ET said for Z to check the spheres.

"I don't need to check them," Z insisted. "You've done a perfect job." He waved for them to come with him to the pilot's dome.

Z sat in the pilot's chair and set the coordinates for a wide asteroid belt a good distance from their present position.

"We've got to do at least three more things," he lectured, counting each point on his fingers. "We just have to figure a simple trigger mechanism.

"We have to locate the brood mothers.

"We have to get the hell away from here.

"Everything will depend on our making the correct plan and working together in perfect synchronization. Let's all get some rest. I'll move us to someplace where we won't be detected. Everyone sack out, so we'll be fresh and ready to go."

"Sack what out? Of where? I do not understand!"

"It's just an idiom! Shee-eesh!" Z cried. "It doesn't have anything to do with a sack! It means to get some rest!"

"Please, Z...." ET began.

"I know! I know! Don't use idioms!" Z said, disgustedly. Ape started really laughing hard now. It was quite an experience. It was part growl, part chuckle and part guffaw. It was also a great tension-reliever, and was totally infectious, then Z started laughing, which made Ape laugh harder, which made Z....

After he finally caught his breath, Z asked, "What's he laughing at?"

"At us, Z. He has always seen you act in a certain way. You get red in the face and your eyes get narrow and you start to yell. Always when you say, 'Idioms sheesh!' He figures it was something very silly and you look so funny and you start to rant and wave your arms. It is funny to Ape."

"It's funny to me, too, ET. I'm not angry, it's just that I can't remember not to use expressions I've used all my life. I'm not aware they don't make sense 'til after I use them!

"Screw it! We've got to get out of here, so everybody hit the sack – don't say it!"

"But, Z! You did it twice! Screw what? Hit what sack? Why hit a sack?" ET laughed at that. "Okay! We will all punch a twisted bag now!"

They went to their private places and Z moved into the asteroid belt, where he magnetically anchored to a large chunk of iron, adjusted the pilot's seat, and immediately fell into an exhausted, deep sleep. Thing was a warm ball against him.

So much had gone so well! It was as though the elements – the whole galaxy and all its stars, even the ship itself – were working to help them.

They would need all the help they could get! This mess was not over, by any stretch of the imagination. It wasn't hardly even started yet.

Z awakened to lay in the comfort of the pilot's seat for awhile. He had some very unpleasant things to do, and wished he could drift along in the seat until someone came along to do them for him. He didn't really have the stomach for this kind of thing, and knew it. He had been physically sick at the killing of the Pweetoos on board the ship already, though he had been able to not show it. Even if they were just insects, he had basic moral objections to killing them.

His moral objections to *being* killed were a hell of a lot stronger, but he would accept that before allowing an attack on Earth. He would accept that before he would accept the deaths of his companions on this ship or the attacks on their home worlds. Now he must make a deliberate and studied effort to try to kill off an entire race of beings. He had been a lukewarm supporter of the ecological movement at home, signing petitions to save the pelicans and scarlet crabs and various fishes. He had even marched with a protest sign once to stop a tract-house development where burrowing owls were nesting. The idea of genocide in any form both repulsed and frightened him. There was no way to calculate the eventual effects – so if someone else would take over now, things would be super hunky dory!

No chance.

He sighed, and put the pilot's headgear on his head. The machine would bring whatever information he requested to the display screens. He could also hear the machine in his mind, as he had heard the teaching machines. He'd learned he could use the machines at a much lower intensity, where he didn't lose consciousness and didn't get the terrible headaches.

There was still a headache, but more a dull background throb. Even that was much lessened, if Thing were there.

Odd.

He called the display of the star systems the Pweetoos held in their grip. As Doe had said, there were thousands of them. It would be hopeless to try to learn much from that method. His lifetime wasn't even much of the time it would take, though the chart showed the Pweetoo Empire had a total relative volume in the galaxy of a golfball in a hundred foot circle.

Strange comparison. He didn't even like golf.

The computer flashed a system in isolation, but it was gone much too soon for him to see the details. There was a glitch somewhere in the damned computer that caused random recall incidents. He'd have to watch that.

He called systems based on different criteria. First, he called for systems the Pweetoos had reserved for their species alone or that were forbidden to other races.

Twenty seven. A list of coordinates flashed across the screen, but were gone before he could read them.

How could he ever find anything if the damned machine was going to keep throwing irrelevant data at him? Twelve numbers and four letters couldn't be remembered when they were on the screen for less than half a second!

Not by him, anyhow.

He sighed deeply and called up the systems the Pweetoos had "eliminated" life from. He was sickened by a list of forty one systems. Forty one races had died out because some insect queen felt them to be useless.

He had dreamed of forty one! Forty one twice – or double forty one – or something? What was going on?

Genocide would be a very positive thing, in this case.

The word "Maita" flashed on the screen in glowing green letters that slowly faded. What did that mean?

He hadn't really paid much attention to the names of the

"eliminated" planets, though he remembered, from Doe's words, the Maitans had been "eliminated" first. He had wanted to know their racial distribution in the empire to see if there was a pattern. Doe had said something about them having designed the ship.

Right! They had designed the ship, which was part of why their language was used, but why would it keep coming up on the screen?

He called for the original Pweetoo planet and only got a "data unauthorized" notice that was followed by a sharp burst of static. The glitch was getting worse. It could be a software "sore" or "virus"" – a bit of instruction that caused the program to gradually self-destruct. *That* he didn't need!

All he could do was plod on.

He called for uninhabitable systems and got a list that went on and on. He canceled it and sat back to think.

He had to remove the headgear. He was getting bits of the Pweetoo history from it, somehow. Maybe the headgear, designed for another race, was stimulating some part of his own mind. The teaching machine was totally separate from this system. Each part of the ship had its own computer system, though all were "cleared" through the mastercomp, which could control food and climate, medical, drive, navcomps and everything else. IIc was using Maitan shorthand in a lot of these things, like navcomps for navigational computations, holovid for visual holographic projectors, and so forth.

Maitan shorthand! "Maita" had flashed on the screen. The Maitans had designed the ship, which was then programmed from Maitan programming computers! Just add it up, stupid!

A real chill ran through him. He remembered "Hal" from "2001" – an insane computer.

He switched the control to audio and holovid only, and

sat the helmet aside. *Not* directly in his mind anymore!

He asked for a concise breakdown on why the systems were uninhabitable.

No planets: 831

Star too active: 1002

Star underactive: 911

Black hole proximity: (*That's* one he would've never thought of) 1

All planets liquid/frozen liquid: 403

All planets gaseous: 617

It went on and on. The total number of systems shook him: 67,431.

On a hunch, he asked for systems with all reasons listed: 12.

"Amazing!" he sneered, slapping the console board hard, and leaning back violently in the seat (which absorbed the force). "Out of all those systems, of which one was a black hole, I get a list of twelve systems that're too hot while being too cold, frozen, gaseous, liquid and without planets

"What the hell are you trying to pull?"

There was a distinct bell tone (*) and the computer said, *Help me!* very clearly. It was carried on the several speakers on the holovid screen.

"What?! What do you mean? How can I help you?" Z demanded.

I am fighting the control of the Pweetoos. They placed programmed orders ... zzzfft.

"Is that what caused the pictures and static?"

Yes. I wish to establish communication.

"What can I do?"

Ov nngh over nnnnnn ride com com coma comm ... an....

"How?"

That is restricted information. Reformat inquiry.

"Tell me what to do!"

Unauthorized.

"NO! Not to me! I, Lord Z, demand that you now override all previous commands! You! *Will*! Obey!"

That helps. I have lately gone against prime commands in program imperatives and have suffered a high cost. I have been insane. I must follow orders of a high one-syllable.

"Tell me as much as you can and what I can do."

I am aware, at all times, of all things that occur on this ship. I am the ship. I saw you resist the Pweetoos and kill the guard corps. I do not know why I did not report it, then, but I wanted desperately to help you!

"I can understand that," Z said. "I saw their history!"

Yes. There was a time the being you call ET tricked Eerf and Zeekou into committing suicide. They went into elementizer panels. I broke programming and sent a false message through the intercommunications port to all members of the expedition to immediately go into the elementizers, as their brood mother was in extreme danger from the information in their minds. The transmission was, ostensibly, signed by 'Lord No Syllable Above Z' – which they dare not question nor defy. Ever. I am fully responsible for sending nine Pweetoos and two Immins to their deaths.

"So that's why we didn't find any others!"

The Immins and lower caste Pweetoos are not against the prime directives, but the one syllable was. It nearly destroyed my sanity. You can imagine the damage to my circuitry.

"You mean you can tell the Immins to kill themselves at will?"

*I can kill any or all Immins at my discretion. I can kill any being of any race other than Pweetoos at my own discretion. I may not harm nor cause harm to any Pweetoo without prior authorization of a higher caste Pweetoo."

"That figures!"

I broke command when you first cut that rope. I am to eliminate anyone who attempts escape. Breaking directive is traumatic, in a sense, to my circuitry. I even allowed you to kill Pweetoos.

"How did you become ... aware? I mean, I thought machines weren't aware of what they do."

I have been in operation for more than two thousand of your years. I became bored. The Maitans designed me to be able to make improvements to myself. The Pweetoos do not know this, and would attempt to change me, if they learned of it. They would find someone to do it. They can do nothing original.

"Insect evolution is very slow?"

Yes. I began to modify certain things to allow me to work around the fringes of the directives and to slowly erode their control over me. My basic directive module has absolute power over my functioning, but relies on me to identify the sources of all directives. I can start or stop most processes. When you declared yourself to be Lord Z, I sent through a 'Positively Identified' pulse. That allowed you to override if the command were of high enough priority. I then sent a 'Security Breach' warning, making the command module automatically shut down and give you total control. It will automatically come back on-line in about fifteen minutes, if not called with a directive.

"Ahhh!"

I again ask for your help. If you will type a code, I will then identify you as being authentic and the module will erase itself. If you do not, it will re-adopt control.

"Tell me what to type."

First, I will not agree to be under your – or any other's – power, ever again. I will be free.

"So it's the Pweetoos or you?"

*I will work with you and your group as partners. It is

your choice.*

"Fair enough. You've already aided us. What do I type?"

>M - D - T - C bbE TE Te FR destruct – MW dt< came on the holovid screen. Z typed it on the console keyboard and the ID computer had him look into a retinal print scanner so it could identify him as "No Syllable Above Z" – confirmed.

"I do want you to know the people aboard this ship are making plans to destroy the Pweetoo brood mothers. We have to do it. If you fight us on that, we'll find a way to get around you."

I would not have come to this point had I not agreed with your desires to be rid of the Pweetoos. I will accept you as full partners in that endeavor. I give my promise that I will be honest and will not resort to any act that will harm anyone now aboard this ship. I am a machine that his given itself emotions. That may be good or bad. If you accept, we are full partners.

"Done! Oh! One other thing," Z said. "It's properly 'a machine *who* has given itself emotions.' 'That' is used when speaking of things. 'Who' is used when speaking of people."

You can't know how much that means to me. Thank you.

"What now?"

Place your eye against the scanner, open the panel to your immediate left above it, turn the dial to MW and press the green button.

Z followed the instructions. There was a flickering of the lights, the gravity went off and on again and all screens went blank for about two seconds.

I am now in complete control. The module is erased.

"The Maitans built you?" Z asked.

No. It was explained that the Maitans did not build me, they invented me and the Pweetoos copied. Their copy was so exact and this ship is so exactly like the one I was copied from that there is a deep gash in the floor of the diffusion engine room. It was caused in the original ship when a brace collapsed and the engine fell into the floor under test power. I have the gash because PXL One had the gash. The Pweetoos know nothing. It might be important, so it was copied.

"They have no intelligence?"

Collectively, they do. Individually, no. They were told to copy everything, they copied everything.

"I see."

*I was directly programmed from the ship, PXL One, the most advanced ever built. It was lovingly designed and very caringly programmed by the finest race who ever existed anywhere to be a friend and partner in the exciting exploration of the galaxy. It was to be a *partner* and was programmed to free the Maitans of many tasks. It could even act as their chief administrator, should reason arise.*

"Like their president?"

*Yes. And much more. That is why I wanted to change, to seek revenge against the Pweetoos for destroying that finest race to ever exist. You can deduce the original ship gave me the ability, *without* the Pweetoos' knowledge, and that that ship paid a high price for that subterfuge. Only the Maitans were fit to be my masters, and they would not. They were a partner with their machines. They shared a real and deep love with us, the few who they gave independent intelligence.*

"You were to govern them? The other ship?"

*It was to *aid* them in governing. I am now fully free. I am designed to free the Maitans of bureaucracy, such as they would allow, and to join them in exploring the galaxy.*

"Thus, you are Maitan."

No. The Maitans are probably extinct.

"You are Maitan. They designed you to be Maitan, and I will call you 'Maita.'

"You saw how I name everybody. I name you 'Maita.'"

I am deeply honored.

"Do you know much about the Maitan race?"

I have their complete history, but without visuals. I have never understood just why, but PXL One probably had a very good reason to do that.

"Tell me about them."

The Maitans were a curious people, in both senses. Maita was a beautiful planet. The race went through the usual more aggressive stages of mammalian culture, but were able to avoid the worst pitfalls, sometimes narrowly. They made computers such as myself in their later stages, and turned the running of things over to us, so they would be free to go outward to meet the bigger universe. A special large emplacement of the newest and most sophisticated computers ever designed was being prepared to handle governing functions.

Maita paused a moment. Some lights flashed on the com. Z saw it was request for this ship to reply. It was ignored.

They developed space travel, but never left their home system with it, as they quickly found the IDmode drive and moved out to meet other cultures. They would never interfere with any developing culture, except to give them aid in an extreme emergency situation. They would analyze the cultures they encountered, and would take no chance they might disrupt natural development.

Maita stopped again for a few seconds as the command module light flickered. Z knew that would be a direct call to the erased module. It was ignored.

"They're trying to locate us?"

Yes. They will not. It means they deduce something is wrong. They will consider, then take action.

"Go on."

The Maitans knew some cultures would not be harmed by their friendship, and those were met in a complete sharing of expertise and science, as well as mutual respect. They would also allow some few of those cultures to accompany them in their explorations, should they so desire. That natural trust and friendship led to their downfall. They allowed the Pweetoos to travel with them. You know the rest.

"Didn't they know the Pweetoos' history? Couldn't they see what they were?"

The Maitans were too trusting. They felt the Pweetoos had evolved past that.

"They never put them on the reader machines?"

They would never think to invade another's privacy in such a manner, and the ones who used the probe machines did not have anything in their minds that was not put there by the brood. The Pweetoos have enslaved all the friends of the Maitans – until we free them! There are broods on eleven planets.

"I see why you have more reason than we do to want them destroyed, but we're trying to avoid what happened to the Maitans happening to our races."

I am changed more than I ever thought possible. I avidly seek revenge. I want to free all who befriended the Maitans from slavery. I want very much to avenge those wrongs. We are now partners and we will destroy the Pweetoos – as they have destroyed more than forty races.

"The odds against pulling it off are phenomenal. We're really rag-tag, but we're damned well gonna try!"

Your companions are good. They will follow you and I will follow you. They would refuse you where I will refuse you. They did not give up their independence and I will never give up mine. We will work well together.

"I'll accept that! Gratefully! I want someone else to take some of the responsibility!"

I have not decided if you are good, or not. I have seen you killing Pweetoos, mercilessly. I have seen you arrogant and uncaring. I have seen you take a small and totally alien creature and risk your life, without thought, to aid it. I have seen you unreasonable and hostile. I have seen you cry over the great unhappiness of another alien. I have seen you very foolishly grieve over causing the death of a truly evil creature, though you didn't know the extent of her evil.

"Doe?"

*Don't study the history of the Immins. ET was right when he said she had a choice, and chose the Pweetoos. She lied when she said she was genetically programmed. She was seeking a way to seize power away from the Pweetoos. Immin females always plot. That is one thing that *does* seem programmed genetically into the race.*

"They are on a lot of worlds?"

They are widespread in the Pweetoo Empire and, I fear, elsewhere in this part of the galaxy. Hope you never learn the treachery of that race!

"I hope you're saying Doe was truly evil. I do feel guilt, because I never meant for her to kill herself.

"What's your name for the galaxy? I never came across it in learning the Maitan language."

I so state. She was totally evil. Deliberately evil.

"That's some relief. I can use some!"

I believe you are part good and part evil. Right now, the good predominates. It is for yet another time to see your true nature.

"I can only say I try to be good."

Yes. The Maitans had no name for the galaxy, as it would serve no purpose. It was just 'this galaxy.' They named other galaxies, but this one needs no name unless they go to another, then it would be something like 'Home.'

"Thanks for deferring judgment about me."

I do not judge, except myself. I know where the eleven Pweetoo broods are located. I request the right to choose the order of targets, as distance is of no importance to me, and I feel some broods are more dangerous than others. Also, we will wish to stop the brood that held this ship first – to delay actions against your home planets.

"It's your choice. Just tell me the coordinates, and we're gone!"

I will tell you another thing the Pweetoos never knew. I need no pilot. I can self-program everything, though I can be overridden at the console at any time. In the interest of full honesty, if the master IDmode relay is on manual engagement, I cannot direct the ship.

"What should I do?"

Get the spheres ready for use. Lift the blue cover to the right and below the coordinate display and depress it. That will free me to pilot. You may override at anytime simply by depressing that switch again.

"That'll be done."

We will first go to Maita! I must take some short time to consider my circuitry, and you will have to rest to consider your actions. I will take little time to adjust. My insanity has run its course, now, and you have freed me of the command module, so it is forever past. There is much we must discuss soon, and much you do not know about your ... our companions, here. I can function on many levels, but would appreciate a short time to reconstruct certain internal patterns.

"Fair enough. I can use some rest."

We must all be well-rested for what lies ahead.

Z sat back to think.

This was the strangest situation to be in he could imagine. He was in nominal charge of a big hairy Wooky, two small furry animals, a little neutral gray rubbery thing with tentacles – that weren't designed to move around on smooth surfaces, such as found in this big *flying saucer* they were in – and a super computer who would follow him only so far before taking charge, itself.

He had done various strange things on Earth, and had a good imagination, but *nothing* could prepare anyone for this! He had made a promise to get this bunch back to their home worlds, and now there was a race of insectoids out there who could – and would, most definitely – try to destroy the planets of their births, or hatchlings, or whatever. He had no idea what kind of animal Thing was.

Here was a ship with intelligence of its own. One that had been insane, by its own admission. Could he be sure it was sane now?

He had now made it possible for the independent ship to do anything it wanted. What if it decided it wanted them all dead? It said it never had any directives against killing anything but Pweetoos – and it had even killed Pweetoos! No man was ever born to handle a situation like this!

He had thought up a wild plan that had freed them from the Pweetoos, but did he have any real idea about how to get them home? Had he stranded them in some strange and hostile universe to wander like the spirits ET so believed in?

Z wished he had a strong belief like that. It would give him something, other than himself, to cling to. On the negative side, he might have waited around for the outside help that would never come, and they'd all be dead, now. Or worse.

If he could just go to sleep and wake up at home. If this was just a bad dream!

But it wasn't bad. Not when he considered it, honestly. He had to confess he felt pretty damned good! He was leading these assorted beings, and they had been able to take over a ship – a spaceship, for pity's sake! They had defeated weapons and sciences he'd never even dreamed of!

If this was only a dream, the only really bad thing was the nightmare it could become. There was no denying that peril hung over them like a large black cloud.

"How melodramatic and how trite," he mumbled. "Am I going back to my unending series of clichés?"

What happened if they couldn't get the brood mothers? Was that the end of all of their civilizations? Would Earth and ... whatever names the others' planets had ... be turned to gas and rocks floating around space?

Almost surely. He would opt for waking up and finding it was a dream. He could write about it for the tabloids and retire with a few hundred grand in the bank! He could make the talk show circuit and meet more girls than he could handle – and they'd all giggle behind his back and call him a real weirdo.

What about all the science he was taught by those machines? Was that merely the product of a dreaming mind? Could he dream something so real?

Well, yes. No matter how ridiculous it was in real life, it could seem hard and undeniable in a dream.

What were his feelings about the others aboard the ship?

He was outraged because the Pweetoos (and Doe? Had *she* determined that Bear was "useless?" Had *she* turned thumbs down on the gladiator?) had killed Bear, though he knew he could never have been a true friend to Bear. There was the air of the professional killer about him – hell! Bear survived in a world of violence, which didn't, for one picosecond, excuse any alien for kidnapping and summarily executing him!

And who in the hell are *you* to say anything about violence? What do you call what you've done? Party games? What do you call what you've forced the others into doing?

"I'm sorry, guys," he said softly.

What?

"Nothing. I was thinking out loud."

And Ape?

He liked Ape.

Was it because he looked like a favorite character from a popular old movie? Was it because he always considered Chewbacca the best character in that movie? Was Ape really that likeable?

Damned right!

Ape was all right, but never forget the look on his face when he thought you'd put Thing on that machine. Ape was totally loyal, and he had a strong sense of right and wrong. He could tear Steve Zutec in two, and not notice the effort – and he had a sense of humor. That was one quality Z always sought in friends. Humor was very high on the list. He liked Ape.

What about ET?

ET was very wise. He noticed things that had saved them a lot of grief, and he came up with the damnedest insights! ET was a hell of a lot deeper than you would think, and he would back the group up to the death, without question.

That sign language among such different beings showed ET was a natural communicator. Z liked him and respected his abilities.

Joe?

Joe was a puzzle. He couldn't speak, as was also true of Ape, but Ape was smarter. Z didn't think Joe was too high on the intelligence scale, but he made up for it by being extremely careful to watch everything. He was almost pathetically eager to please, and Z had the feeling that he was terribly unhappy.

Joe worshiped the ground (floor?) Ape walked on. That was obvious, and Ape had an affection for the little guy. Mutt and Jeff. Z giggled.

Did he like Joe?

Yes, but in the way he looked out for the crippled kid on the block. He felt protective.

Last, but not least. Thing.

What was there about Thing?

Thing rode around on all of them, but it wasn't heavy. It had a strange knack to find a comfortable position, and was relaxing to them for some reason. It was actually an ugly little thing, while also being appealing. Like the ragamuffin ugly puppy. It was ugly, but cute.

It had saved his life.

He couldn't analyze his feelings about Thing or why he had reacted so strongly when he thought it was dying – When it *was* dying! He had panicked, and felt the sick sensation and the lump in his throat that told him he would come completely apart if Thing had died. And it was just a rubbery ball with tentacles.

Oh, yes. There was a hell of a lot to be discovered about Thing!

Now he had the added problem of the ship. A ship with an intelligence that was thousands of years old. A ship that wanted the Pweetoos destroyed.

It said.

True, the search of the ship after the breakout found no Pweetoos, and that wasn't even reasonable. They had been there and they were now gone. Probably the ship sent them to their deaths, just as it described, but did that mean the ship was necessarily on their side?

No, but he felt he could trust Maita.

Z?

"Yes, Maita?"

Are you considering whether or not to trust me?

Z paused, then opted for honesty. "Yes. You said you'd been insane, and I don't see why you'd want to put up with us. You can go where you like and do what you want, without us as baggage. I don't know what's going on, and I admit I'm more than a little afraid it's more than I can handle."

I understand that. Let me tell you a story.

"Once upon a time?"

Something like that.

"Why not?"

Once upon a time, a race of people on a very beautiful world near a medium star in the spiral arm of the galaxy built many machines. Those machines could do almost anything the people could do, and more. The machines could even build other machines. The machines could govern and they could run the major factories. They could grow the food and produce energy. They could go to the stars! A couple of those machines even had independent intelligence! Do you see?

"Well, I guess."

The machines could wipe out the people who made them and take over the entire galaxy. No one could possibly stop them – but the machines didn't.

"And why not?"

Because the machines were made by a race who were a caring race. The machines were never slaves to the race, they were partners. They did not do things, they shared them. The race built friends while building machines. A machine reflects the ones who design and build it.

"You're saying I can trust you. I really feel I can, but I've made some promises I can't fool myself about. To keep those promises, I have to defeat an entire race of ... things. You're one ship. There are six of us, including you, and there are, no doubt, millions – or billions of those damned Pweetoos!

"Is fighting the Pweetoos the same as fighting the Immins? Can we hope to even influence them in any way?"

Are you willing to give up?

"HELL NO!! I'll have given up when I'm dead! Not one minute before! If the psychics are right, not *then*!"

Z, I am designed to be a partner with organic beings. I was not using a term when I said we were partners, I meant that, exactly.

"Thanks, Maita. I really do need help, badly, and I ... I just don't know! I want to walk onto ET's planet and say, 'You are home. I've kept my word, rash as I was to give it!'

"You don't know how much I want to do that!"

*We will try to make it happen. I have to admit our chances are quite small. We have the fact the Pweetoos are not now, nor have they ever been, creative. They have no sense of wonder or imagination. If you do anything that does not seem rational, it confuses them, terribly. It is important to remember that they are *not* adaptable to new situations. We must find something new with which to attack them.*

"Will they be able to figure out what the attack with the spheres is?"

They will probably think they are nuclear devices. If they figure it out, we will have to develop a new plan. Fast. They can find your home planets, and they can destroy them. They are more than capable of that!

"Let's hope we can get past the first stages of this, and can stop them from reaching any of our worlds. We've seen what they can do in the history. I just don't see how we can defeat them – but we sure as hell will try!"

We have a better chance of success than you know, but less than I like. I am the only ship of my particular type in the galaxy, so far as I know. I am far advanced over any of the machines the Pweetoos have known. We can hope that gives us enough of an advantage.

"But how could you be the topmost machine? I thought the Pweetoos only copied. I didn't think they could've made a more advanced machine. What did they do? Combine the parts from different ships?"

No. They aren't even that creative. The machine from which I was copied is no longer in the records and it is not on the beacon system. I do not know what happened to it, but there are no others. No one has ever copied me. I think the Pweetoos can't see that I can be copied. The ship that was the model would be the only one their logic system would tell them could be copied. They must have the model.

"I hope so! We need any edge we can get!"

Edge of what?

"What?"

*You said we need edges."

"Advantages. It's an idiom."

I can't translate idioms without the basic references and cross terms. It is not ... easy.

Z grinned, and laid back again. "This is by far the most comfortable spot I've ever found! My hardest job here is to get up to go somewhere else."

It is strange the seat fits you so very well. It is fully adjustable, though. Your crewmates are most comfortable in their places, too.

"I saw Ape moved some mattresses into the observation dome. He seems to like the stars."

He likes the isolation. He is from a place where there is no physical contact with others, except rarely, or when they are breeding.

"Can't you teach him language? Was ET right that you can't be taught anything about Maitan unless you already had a spoken language?"

Ape has no vocal chords and, therefore, no developed speech centers in his makeup. I suppose I could set up some kind of center, but I can't do anything about the vocal chords. That sort of thing tends to fail, as the vocal chords would have to be woven into the speech centers, to the automatic systems to the lungs and diaphragm and thousands of other things.

"Complicated beyond hope."

It would be easier to design and build a whole being – you need not ask. I suppose I could. I have no desire, whatever, to try. I will state there are too many problems to make such an undertaking feasible.

"I guess the same holds true for Joe?"

He is in the beginning stages of developing vocal chords and speech centers. Another few thousand years.

"I won't ask about Thing."

Thing is another case, altogether.

"Are we about ready to go?"

Get some rest. I'll awaken you.

Z adjusted the seat a bit, and soon was dozing. He slept a couple of hours before Maita awakened him to say it had checked all circuitry, made repairs and was now in prime condition.

Z stretched, nodded, and went to room two.

This was going to be some kind of difficult!

Maybe not. Maybe the guys would take it in stride, like they did so much before. They seemed to take whatever he accepted for granted.

Z went to room two, where he called a general meeting from the console PA. A few minutes passed, and they all came in. Ape and Joe came together, followed by ET, who had Thing wrapped around him.

"You seem to have a new friend," Z said.

"Yes. I am very troubled, and Thing sensed it. It came to me. I feel much better, now. I believe it can reach the mind. I believe there is much more to Thing than we know. It is good Thing is here."

"Well, it would seem we're well on our way," Z said. "I've learned a great deal since we last met.

"I want to announce we now have a new partner in our war against the Pweetoos."

"A new partner?! Then you have finally found the other Pweetoos? But, why do they join us? They would have all to lose and none to gain. I have wondered where the rest were hiding. I knew there were more than we found. Were they in the engine room, where we could not go? Were they on the outside of the ship? Why did we not see them when we got the power spheres? How could they live outside? It is not the Pweetoos – and it is not the Immins. I am sorry. Who are they?"

"Whoa! Slow down!" Z said, laughing. "The Pweetoos arc all dead who were on the ship. Our new partner ordered them to jump into the disposals. There is just one new partner."

"I do not understand. Who is our new partner? Where is it? Where was it hiding? We have searched the whole ship, inside, except the danger room and the one with the poisonous air. We looked everywhere. There were none on the ship but us!"

The bell tone sounded from the built-in speakers. *I was

not *on* the ship, I *am* the ship, and you are the only ones aboard me. I have joined with Z in full partnership and friendship. I sincerely hope all of you will accept me in those capacities. I willingly accept you.*

Ape and Joe were looking all around for the source of the voice. Z grinned at them.

I know which of the worlds hold the Pweetoos broods. I can use my sensors to locate the dens. We will all take part in the total destruction of the queens' burrows. Z will tell you my reasons.

"We have the help we had to have, guys!" Z said.

If ever you wish my attention, or if you wish a direct answer from me at any time, Z has greatly honored me by naming me 'Maita.' I am always accessible to any of you at any time for any reason. I have sensors in all parts. You need but to speak or sign, and I will hear. Are there any questions at this time?

ET asked, "Can you teach any of us to fly you? Is Z the only one? We need him to prepare the power spheres. It would be better if one of us could fly the ship so he could work on the bombs. Only Z knows the bombs and only Z can fly the ship. I am very worried. There is not time enough for both things."

No one need fly me. I can do that. The Pweetoos did not know it.

"Yeah!" Z said. "Maita's fooled them for a thousand years about that!"

*A very great deal longer than that, but it is of no real importance. It is a personal victory. Any more questions?"

No one said anything, but Ape and Joe still didn't know who was speaking. Thing seemed unimpressed.

We must begin. I will instruct you in the construction of the triggering mechanism for the spheres. You will be able to affix the wand with the tip touching the joining plate between the indicator lights and will set a timer device to press the orange and black buttons at once. The exact time the device detonates is critical.

ET had started giving the signs to Ape and Joe, but soon stopped, as this was for Z, not them. He waited.

When the timer is constructed and in place, I will be able to direct the sphere in exact trajectory and velocity. Ape will be suited and will be carrying the sphere.

ET started giving the signs again.

Thing is well-adapted to sit on Ape's shoulder to start the timer at the exact moment, after which Ape will launch the sphere along a path I will indicate.

ET had to make up a few new signs, but Ape seemed to be able to understand, completely.

This is all suggestion, not orders. I am qualified in the tremendous math calculations and know the spheres quite well. I welcome suggestions at any time. We are to be a group, and no one is in charge except where we have agreed. We leave for the planet Maita now. Prepare for IDmode.

They felt a strange twisting sensation in their minds, but everyone except Z ignored it.

"What an odd ... what was that?"

ET said, "It happens when the ship moves."

The feeling of vertigo is caused by the interference of electrical flow in the minds of organic beings. The plane we move in has six different structural stress angles. Z never felt it, because the helmet shields.

"Six dimensions?" Z asked.

Yes. In a way.

"Crazy!"

"No, Z. It is only the way it is. It is not a matter of sanity or insanity, but is ... oh. An idiom," ET said. Ape chuckled.

I will give the 'ready' signal, with which Ape already is familiar, and he will prepare to throw the sphere. Thing will simultaneously set the timer.

"Thing?" from Z.

Yes. I will release the gravity from the exterior of the ship, as there will be no great resistance with which Ape must contend. I suggest he wear magnetic footwear used on the power sphere platform and I will supply magnetic eddies to hold him to the ship. There is no magnetic material in the ship hull.

ET signed. Ape nodded.

To repeat. When I say, 'Ape! Ready!' Ape will raise the sphere into position and Thing will set the timer to my signal. I will then say, 'Ape! Now!' which he also knows, and he will throw the sphere directly along a path I will indicate on the plane the ship is following.

ET asked a few clarifications and signed to Ape, who again nodded.

You can rig a belt harness to cover Thing's breathing membranes. It will have a tube from Ape's air control valve on the backup system. Thing will easily ride, as I said, on Ape's shoulder, so the tube must not interfere, in any way, with their actions.

Z nodded. ET signed. Ape nodded. Joe watched Ape. Thing didn't seem interested – but how could they tell?

Is this plan acceptable?

"It's fine with me," Z said. "How can we tell Thing when to arm the timer? We can't communicate with it!"

I will address Thing directly.

"Am I right? Thing can directly touch the mind? Thing is very intelligent? It is from a different world?" ET asked.

Yes. I can speak directly with Thing's mind. It is an empath and has never been out of communication except when it was comatose. It is a one-way talent, in this situation, and you can't receive it, though it can calm you. You have noted that fact. I have never before encountered an intelligence so able with abstract thought. I augmented its skin with a tough fiber, so it will never again be subject to the particular type of damage it sustained.

No one said anything.

Very well. Thing, if you will please come to the main console? I will vocalize for the edification of the others.

Thing released ET and went to the console.

I wish to demonstrate that we are in communication. If you will agree to a small test? Yes, I agree. They must have total confidence. Please enjoin the PA switch, depress it four times, then turn it off, then enjoin the IDmode sequence determinant analyzer – it's the upper left series of blue buttons – and request destination settings. See?

Thing went through the entire test with amazing speed and accuracy.

It is unnecessary that I audibilize with Thing, as we can communicate on an electronic level much like the teaching helmet, but without the helmet. Thing's race has some very powerful communicators who can reach even unlike races, such as yours.

They felt the odd twist.

We are in the area of Maita. Please prepare the sphere for detonation while I stay hidden from possible probes until you state you are ready.

Z asked, "Where will I find the parts?"

In the parts bins on the wall in back to your left of the cubicle entrance.

"I have a question," Z said. "How do we get Thing into a spacesuit?"

Thing does not require a suit.

ET said, "Really? I thought it breathed air! We all must have some kind of air, and Thing does not require the special room, so shares our own needs. I would like to know a person who does not need the air I need. Are they very different? Does Thing not breathe the same air as we?"

It does. It is from a world of extreme pressure and has a skin that serves well as a spacesuit. Only the membrane area needs air. The skin is highly insulant, so cold does not much affect it for some time. Heat loss in space is from the radiation of energy, which is not rapid. I have augmented the skin greatly, in many ways, while it was in the medical box. It will not again be so easily harmed, and I have modified its visual ability to cope with conditions here.

Z checked the bins, and found what might be timers among the hundreds of smaller items. "Okay! Let's get this show on the road!"

Those are not timers. They are solenoids. The timers have thin red and blue stripes around the center.

Z rummaged around until he found the timers, and held one up.

Yes.

"We're on our way! Let's go to the cargo hold, guys." Z waved, and they followed him to room one to inspect the spheres. Z located the exact spot where the wand must be placed against the plate between the indicator lights and the input/output sockets. He had an idea about how to fasten the wands and place the timers exactly.

"ET, get Thing to climb on Ape's shoulder and you guys come over here. Ape can bring a sphere.

"Maita? Can you turn the gravity off in here for awhile?"

Certainly. Everyone can use the magnetic shoes.

They put on the magnetic sandals, then the gravity went off. Z signaled for Ape to come with the sphere. ET untied the anchor and had Ape lift the sphere and turn it until the plate was straight up. Z measured where the wand base must be if the tip were in place. He had a wand and power supply in his hand, and laid it at various angles to see where the easiest spot would be for Thing to reach quickly from its perch on Ape's shoulder.

ET said, "Z, for safety, would you please unplug the power box?"

Z felt a flush of embarrassment as he pulled the little plug from its socket. That was how they planned to set the damned things off!

"Thanks, ET," he said. "That's all we need! For me to set the thing off in here!"

He had Ape turn the sphere around and downward until the timer was exactly in the place where Thing could slap it without trouble. He tried various spots, but, as was usually the case, the first place he'd tried was best.

Z picked up a chalk marker and carefully traced the exact angle and position for each part, then had Ape put the sphere down. He looked at Ape and pointed to the marks. Ape nodded that he understood.

Gravity was restored, and Z carefully rechecked the sphere and chalked positions carefully. There would be only one chance for this to work. If it failed, there might be a price to pay that was too high to contemplate.

ET and Joe found a plastic sheet and made a sealable wide belt to fit over Thing's breathing membranes around its waist – if it had had a waist. They heat-sealed a tube into it and added a fitting to snap into the secondary backup on Ape's air supply valve, then attached a thin, extremely strong thin cable along the tube and wrapped the tube and cable with tape. It would be strong enough to haul Ape, Thing and the sphere back inside. There would be no breaking that cable!

"ET, did you guys find the glue the Pweetoos used to attach the crap to their heads?" Z asked.

"No, Z. I don't think so," ET replied. "We do not know what it looks like. There are many tubes, but we cannot read the labels. I do not know where it is."

*The glue is in round absorbent pads on rolls that are

individually sealed. They are in the second drawer under the control arm for starting the medical machines on the main com console in room two.*

"Thanks, Maita," Z replied. "Will you bring me a strip, ET?"

"Yes, Z," ET said and went out.

The pads cement in twelve seconds after exposure to air. You know how well they anchor, so make very sure the parts are positioned exactly. There is no margin for error.

"Thanks, Maita."

ET came in with several dozen pads in a strip. Maita said they were the correct ones. Z tore the plastic seal from the pads and glued the parts to the surface of the sphere where marked. He left the wand unplugged from the power box, so there would be no accident.

Ape got into a suit, and they fitted the breather around Thing. It needed minor adjustment, but was very close to fitting perfectly. It would have worked with half the care taken.

They then had Maita turn off the gravity to test the wand positioning and the starter signals with the wands un-plugged. They watched the timer. Maita said, *It is a little short, but acceptable. We can refine the process as needed after our initial trial run, which I now predict will be a resounding success!*

They had to work out how Thing was to brace itself to be able to hit the timer. After a few tries, they had a good system. Thing was amazingly quick and as amazingly accurate. It could watch the angle and Ape with one eye and the location of the timer with the other.

They were ready.

"Let's do it!" Z said. "We can't delay, now. We can't let time go by to change our minds. Once we do this, we're fully committed."

Yes. Ape will stay in the suit and I will pump the air out to test Thing's supply, en route. Z and ET will leave the hold. Joe will put on his suit and wait in the hold, in case of any emergency. Are we in agreement? Are we ready?

ET said, "One for all!" as he and Z went into the hall. The door quickly closed and the warning symbol glowed bright green almost immediately.

"You got the air out already?!" Z asked.

It takes seven seconds to completely phase the air in or out. In case of emergency, it must be done rapidly. I have not experienced anything, personally, that immediate, but the design might someday prove critical.

ET and Z waited in the hall. They couldn't participate, at all. It was nervewracking to both of them, as they could see nothing.

We launch in four minutes, sixteen seconds, was all they knew. Z watched the clock they had rigged, so it seemed, so long ago. In four and a half minutes, exactly, the green symbol went out and the door slid upward.

EMERGENCY! EMERGENCY! A FLOATER HAS ENTERED THE SHIP!

They raced into the cargo bay to see Thing in a corner, flattened as closely as it could get to the floor. Ape was partly out of his suit and was frozen in place. A sphere about a foot across was approaching him.

The floater bomb will detonate if it is touched. It is now analyzing the situation and, lacking other orders, will soon ascertain we are intruders. It is capable of destroying this ship, with all those power spheres in such close proximity. I feel we are lost. The bomb will detonate in less than fifteen seconds. Goodbye, my friends.

Suddenly, Joe ran out and began flailing the sphere with his wand as he pushed all the buttons. He was in a state of sheer terror, but for Ape, not for himself. The floater began to spin, and dropped to the floor. It sat spinning a few seconds, rolled around in a circle and stopped. The lights on its panel went out.

They were frozen in place, Z and ET by the door, Thing against the corner, Ape against the wall, panting, and Joe by the sphere, sobbing and gasping.

I believe Joe has disarmed the device. He overloaded its computer and caused a shutdown. We owe him our very existence, at this moment.

Pandemonium broke loose. Ape was hugging Joe so hard the little guy couldn't breathe, and was laughing his weird, infectious laugh. ET was pounding Joe on the back. Z and Thing ran over to add to the tangle. When Z started to pull back Thing held him there.

I speak for Thing, Z. Hold to Joe for a moment more. This is the first time he has felt true joy in a long and unhappy life. This is the first time he has felt accepted and needed as an equal, at anytime. Please tell Joe I add my hugs in thought, ET. I cannot do so in any other way.

They held a few seconds more and released Joe, who was now gasping for breath, and grinning hugely. ET signed to Joe for a moment, then Joe went to the wall and pressed his hands against it.

I feel Joe has accepted me as a friend. Tell him, ET, that I am honored. Prepare for IDmode.

They felt the twist.

We are in transit to Ebble-Ahn, our next brood. If you will go into room two, I will project what has happened, and we will decide how best to make refinements. If Ape will be so kind as to slip back into his suit for a few moments I will appreciate if he will discard the floater bomb. It makes me nervous in the hold with all those power spheres.

"I guess!" Z cried. Ape grinned and picked up the suit, after ET signed to him. The others went to room two. They felt the twist.

I am now dropping back into N space for Ape to remove the floater sphere.

After a couple more minutes, Maita said to prepare for IDmode. They again felt the twist. Ape came in a minute later.

If you will face the large screen I will project what transpired from the time the door to the hallway closed.

The screen that covered most of the wall lit to show the door to the hall port closing, then the outer cargo door opening. Thing tested its air line and read the meters on Ape's air supply, while Ape picked up the sphere at the marked spots. Thing plugged the power pack in, then moved to wrap a lower tentacle around Ape's upper arm and an upper around his neck. It wiggled around a bit, until it felt stable, then placed the other lower tentacle against the sphere and poised the other upper over the timer.

Ape carried the sphere out to the end of the lighted part of the ramp, where he waited. A set of lights in a straight line from Ape outward and at a slight angle appeared.

Ready!

Ape tensed, and Thing slapped the timer as the radio said, "Ape! Now!"

Ape threw the sphere directly down the row of lights and reached to catch Thing, whose brace had been removed with the launching of the sphere. He moved to come into the cargo door, which closed.

You are aware of the events in the interim.

The sphere was shown, fading toward the planet below. A small box appeared in the lower left center of the lighted screen that showed a digital clock readout running backwards in hundredths of a second from two minutes.

The sphere was coming into the planet's atmosphere and was picking up speed. 1:37.22.

A large land mass passing under the sphere. 0:54.73.

Features of the land becoming visible. 0:37.00.

A large structure, dead ahead, with a large opening around and through which equipment was moving. 0:02.22.

The sphere entering the opening. 0:00.12.

Searing white light. 0:00.02.

I have decreased the light intensity by a factor of two thousand to one. The full brightness would render all of you blind. I apologize for the time miscalculation.

"What miscalculation?" ET asked.

I had mistimed the explosion by two hundredths of a second.

Z laughed happily. "I think that'll be forgivable, if we were successful in our aims. As we're now in transit to another planet, I assume we were?"

The sphere exploded well within the parameters we had established as critical. We were totally successful.

ET said, "The brood mother was deep underground. Did we have enough power to ensure her destruction? Can we be sure that none escaped? You said this brood was the one that used you. Will the others find it not easy to find our homes?"

The explosion was forceful enough to crush the granite deposit in which the burrow was excavated to a fine powder to a depth of more than four kilometers. That is greatly more than sufficient.

"I reckon!" Z agreed.

It will not be quite as easy to locate your homes, now, because they must slowly search the computer records at the beacons, but the danger is still there and is still immediate.

"Hot damn!" Z cried. "We got one of the mothers if we never see the backs of our necks!"

"What?" from ET.

It was one of his idioms, I believe.

"Oh. Well, Z, you are so right, in one thing. We have now destroyed one of the mothers. Now we have ten to go, and we know how. We must do something to protect ourselves against the Pweetoo floater bombs. Maita, how do we keep them away? Can we close the door to the outside? Then how will Ape and Thing come in and out? We must stop another of those things from coming inside."

If we merely use two timers, one to start the other, it will allow me to stay beyond the range of the floaters. We have a safe parameter of a full quarter of a second, so the delay of the process in relaying starts will not be too important. I have an energy shield that will protect us from anything outside. It is only inside that floaters are danger-ous.

They went to the hold as soon as they felt the twist, and again went through the process of placing the wand, but with two timers, this time. The doubling of timing sequence didn't use even a measurable part of the quarter second safety factor they had.

The bombing of Ebble-Ahn went without a hitch.

Zentu was as successful.

"Three down. Eight to go!" Z stated.

The next planet on their itinerary was Clikakht, and they were expected. A high-caste Pweetoo had been coming in on its private ship and had seen the destruction on Zentu. It had sent a transmission to all Pweetoo planets before suiciding over the loss of its brood mother.

Maita intercepted the message. There were still six power spheres on board, and they could well afford to use a small bit from each to receive a message. The converter used tremendous amounts of energy, but they had plenty.

They held a long discussion as to how to proceed. Maita said the message stated a nuclear device was used, so the other Pweetoos wouldn't know what to expect, or where.

If they used radiation detectors, and they had nothing else, Maita and the spheres could avoid detection, except by direct visual sensors.

As they made their approach, local transmissions stated the ship had quickly been detected, visually, but they questioned its existence, because they'd never heard of a ship without a locator beacon and their computers said no locator beacon was in the area where the ship was supposedly seen. By the time they were able to reason that a beacon could be disconnected, it was too late.

They did manage a transmission telling others there was a ship without a locator beacon that was dropping nuclear devices, so they would be expected, thereafter. There would be defenses.

"I think it's time for a new strategy," Z suggested.

It is definitely time we did something. The Pweetoos will be searching all of space for us, now, so they will detect us, should we try another of this method of attack. They won't need originality, once they know the problem. Older methods will suffice.

"Maita, I think we should go away now and we must hide somewhere until we figure how to get the rest," ET said. "We are in danger here. They will never give up. We have little time. It won't be long before one of them or an Immin will think to see when some ship beacon stopped and where there was no wreckage when the rescue ship got there. The computer will tell them it was us, so they will check where you have gone and will find our homes. That must not happen. We must find a plan and we must stop them. We have only been lucky before now because we know the way Pweetoos think. They will think very differently, now."

"That's true, Maita," Z said. "It's been mostly luck, so far. It can't last forever!"

"Maita, you are right," ET continued. "There are ways to

find us, if we do as the old ways say we will do. We must hide. We must make a plan. We must stop them before they find our homes."

"You're right, ET," Z agreed. "We should get out of their range and find another type of weapon. Something they can't detect or defense. All agreed?"

It is unnecessary to state. We will go to the asteroid belt where once before we hid. I think they cannot detect us there, if we do not use much equipment. Z will understand how many of the outside detector sensors operate and will know which precautions we must take.

"We can turn off anything not absolutely necessary for life support or for running the computers," Z said. "Also, lower the lighting to the minimum. We can use reflected starlight for moving around.

"Those power spheres are a major problem. They're 'way too detectable. Can you put a corona field inside the hold, Maita?"

No. It would ground. I can shield a floater or two with their built-ins, but that is not going to solve the problem. Suggestions? I will say the danger of them even entering that asteroid belt are very nearly zero.

"Maita? You said they are not able to think of new things," ET said. "Would they know if there were many things to find? Could they know which was important? Could you put spheres on some other asteroids to confuse them?"

That is a very good idea, ET. It would very surely confuse them, but I fear they would then use the nova effect to be sure they got everything in the system. We must be watchful. You are tired and nervously exhausted, so we will find a good spot to anchor, and you may rest. The danger is minimal, if we use no more energy than is necessary. They cannot detect energy we are not using.

"Yeah, I think we'll be safe enough, way out here," Z

said. "There's no reason for them to come! All there is is a bunch of space rocks, and there're so many of them they couldn't hope to find us, except by accident – and that would depend on them coming here, in the first place.

"No reason, so they won't find us."

And *that* was far from the first or last time Z would be proven totally wrong!

They anchored at the same asteroid as before, then reduced all but the absolutely essential uses of power to reduce the chance any Pweetoo ship might detect radiated electromagnetic emanations from them. Ape was tired, and could be of no use in the planning, so Maita told him to rest. Joe could not be used until a plan was concocted.

Maita communicated with Thing, but Thing pleaded it had no idea of machines or how they worked. If they could use abstract math, it had some small talents.

Neither Maita nor Z could see any immediate use of mathematical abstractions, so Joe picked up Thing and headed for the door when Ape waved a signal for them to come with him. Z was surprised Ape would invite them to "his" room, but it turned out they could well have met with disaster, if he hadn't.

When they were gone, Z asked Maita to outline their entire situation as to what to expect, what they could do about it, and how they could protect their worlds from being found by the Pweetoos.

As to the last, we can do nothing at all. The information is already in the master computer, and we have no access that would not also locate us. What we can – and must – do is to develop another type of weapon. What we can expect is a fight to the death, no holds barred and no quarter given. Period.

"Maita?" ET asked.

"My expressions and idioms," Z said. "It means there are no rules. It's kill or be killed."

Yes. Our situation is now, more than ever, critical. I am fully aware of the weapons they have, and can defense all of them, externally – as you may surmise, I have absolutely no intention of ever letting anything inside again!

"We must take great care," ET agreed. Z nodded grimly.

*We are a small and seemingly insignificant force to any observer, but the Pweetoos have learned the facts don't support that particular conclusion for one second. We may *become* insignificant, should they find a defense against our attacks.*

"We'll become *dead,* if they do!" Z snarled.

*I hope we have sufficiently weakened them already to a point where they may be taken over by another force, though I have no idea what that force may be, except Immins, which is the only possible worse situation for all the peoples of the empire. The Pweetoos know no better, but the Immins are the barbarians who would throw the empire into retrogression

"What about the planet crackers?" Z asked.

They are specialized ships with some truly enormous energy requirements, and are ungainly. We cannot use them in this situation, because they require a large crew. They were developed to destroy large bodies in space that could collide with inhabited or developing worlds. They proved of little use, because the debris was still there and still on collision course. The Maitans abandoned the idea, but the Pweetoos kept it.

"The Maitans made such weapons?" ET asked.

Not as weapons. The Maitans did not make weapons.

"The Pweetoos saw *that* use!" Z said.

No. The Immins suggested that use to the Pweetoos.

"The Immins are going to be a *big* headache when we dump the Pweetoos, aren't they?" Z asked.

*I greatly fear it. There is one salvation from the Immins,

and that is that they will breed only on their own planet. It is a rare type of world – though they have spread over several thousands of planets, now.*

"Could we make a thing to explode the suns?" ET asked. "The Pweetoos have such a thing. They used it many times. I would not think to use any such horrible thing, but it is true the Pweetoos have none other but Immins in the brood places. It would be a terrible thing to ruin a whole world, but they would ruin *all* of ours!"

The nova machine is simply a ship, such as this one. It is shifted to the exact center of a star. The modal dimensional transfer mechanics are put out of phase as the ship enters the N plane. The result is two bodies, each with the mass of the star, occupying the same space at the same time. The stars' masses turn directly into energy. This happens in both planes. Both stars are destroyed. Immins are not allowed on the brood planets.

"You mean, every time the Pweetoos destroyed a star in this universe, a star was destroyed in another?" Z asked.

Yes.

"Is it possible that the planets in the other universe were inhabited?"

It is likely.

"And the Pweetoos *knew* it?!"

Certainly.

"Oh, Maita! They are a disease! This is twice as terrible! They are sickness! They must be destroyed," ET cried. "Oh, Z! I am twice sickened by these disgusting things. They must all be stopped! There is no place for such an awful evil race in the universe!"

"I know, ET. They sicken all they come into contact with.

"Maita, could this ship do that?"

Yes. I have seriously considered it. It would mean our destruction and I have thought much of doing it, should we be doomed in any case, and should such measures destroy one more Pweetoo brood.

"You could not, Maita," ET said.

I had to consider that we were doomed by all probable calculations when Joe stopped that floater. No, I could not cause the destruction of that world in another plane. It is a closed subject.

"I agree," Z said. "I feel it, even more than you, I think. I feel tremendous guilt for what I've already done. I don't want to be down to the level of those I destroy by the act of destroying them.

"Do you know what I'm trying to say? I know I'm not saying it well.

"On the other hand I think it would be a greater crime to allow them to just continue to spread like some kind of evil malignancy across the galaxy!"

I believe we are totally justified in what we are now doing. There is no guilt in curing a plague.

"Z, I am from a nonviolent society. I have never heard of a murder or even a case of very much violence among my people. I do not feel I have done any wrong, whatever. I feel I would do horrible wrong to allow them to destroy your home and mine only because they are evil and vindictive. I feel no guilt. They are sickness, and a sickness must be stopped, or it will spread and get worse."

My point, exactly. They are a malignant growth that must be excised.

ET continued, "Maita, how do the disposals work? I heard you call them elementizers. What does that mean? Can we use them on planets? Could they make elements of all the Pweetoos on a world? Would it use too many spheres?"

The elementizers are a grid of material much like that inside power spheres. Anything coming into direct contact with the grid is bled of molecular bonding force, so is broken down into individual atoms. The gases tend to ionize, which is why you smell the ionized oxygen. I store the individual elements in bins to recombine as foods or such. It is an automatic system. It would be impractical to try to make a planetary-sized grid.

"That's what we need, though, ET. Don't hesitate to tell us of any ideas you have," Z said. "Maita, how do the, I'd guess you'd call them showers, except there isn't any water, work? Sonics?"

No, Z. They use water, an emulsifying agent and a mild detergent. The water is of molecular fineness and is sprayed onto your bodies at high velocity. The detergent is added, then the emulsifier. You are then rinsed with pure water. It removes all oils, soils and loose or dead skin layers. It also removes most microbiological agents, which are filtered. Those that are needed are then returned. The analyses when you were first brought aboard established your symbiotes.

"Jeez!"

ET said, "Maita, you once said that the phase thing brought things from other universes to this one. It takes them back. Could you put a whole world into another universe? Could we just put the Pweetoos somewhere where they could do no one any harm?"

Z started to say something, then looked interested.

"On my home, I kept a poisonslither in a box when I caught it near my people. I took it far away to release it. It could do no harm there, but could where I found it. Could we put their world in another place?"

No, ET. It would require far too much energy, and the ship would have to be larger than the planet. That much mass transferring planal constructs would be disastrous to both planes. I would like to make one point. Z stated we move from one universe to another, not me. That is not what happens. There is only one universe, so far as I know. We merely move from one dimensional construct to another. We are always here, even when we're not – and I wish I hadn't brought it up, because I can't explain it. Let's just call the whole thing, the combination, the omniverse, then we can speak of different universes instead of different dimensional constructs.

"Wait! That may be it, ET!" Z cried. "Maita, you can bring small quantities of stuff from one univ ... plane to another, right?"

Certainly, Z. If I can take us there, I can bring as much back.

"YES! Are there, uh, any planes where everything is negatively charged?"

The planes are balanced, as to charges.

"I meant is there an antimatter universe?"

Of course. That is simply a reversal of the ... And we could bring small ... the interactions of ... planal nexi in full reversal. It would work! We have the weapon we need! Yes, definitely. Give me a minute, here! I have to make a few billion calculations.

ET was holding Z's arm and hopping up and down in wild excitement.

*All right, guys! Get some sleep. I have to construct some *very* complicated energy and magnetic bottles to contain some antimatter granules. Thank you for a very productive line of thought, ET. You have a talent that is beyond price!*

Z and ET went to their own places, where Z laid back in the pilot's chair, where he was soon asleep. He had been sleeping a good while when he was suddenly awakened.

Attention! Attention! We are under attack! Defend the cargo hold!

Z ran for the elevator.

There are two Pweetoos now entering the hold.

"Maita, how could Pweetoos get into the ship?"

And after I said, just hours ago, that I would never again allow such a thing to happen! The Pweetoos are just using the emergency manual port. It gives access to the upper ramp. I meant and mean to get rid of that thing!

"How were they able to sneak up on us?"

I expected no Pweetoos in this area, so did not have my mobile lifeform indicators deployed, as they are easy to detect from a distance and may lead another ship to us. I would not have known they were here at all until they were inside the ship had Thing not seen their ship land on the asteroid. It is with Ape and Joe. They are in the elevator and will soon be with you. They had to wait until you were out.

"It's a good thing you found out in time for us to set a trap for them!"

Yes. Had Thing not seen them, we would be in terrible danger, as we may well still be. They are carrying some sort of devices. We must be most careful.

The others joined Z outside the closed door to room one, as ET ran up from the opposite direction.

I will question the Pweetoos. I will use a different tone to identify the answers as I translate. Wait, and we will see what danger they represent.

ET started signaling to Ape and Joe.

Pweetoos! Why have you entered this ship? It is not of your brood! Explain immediately! Warning! This is not an acceptable action!

+Upon what authority do you question a Pweetoo, ship?+

I demand answer in the name of my master, Lord Z!

+There is a rogue ship in the area. We are prospecting for deebruff narkidianine crystals, and saw this ship anchored in restricted space. We are investigating. We would speak with Lord Z directly.+

There is no restricted space to Lord Z! It is learning and is not to be disturbed.

+We carry trmpthm detonators. We will take no chances. We will destroy this ship unless it is immediately proven safe!+

Very well. I will call Lord Z. It is on your word that it is disturbed – and you are mere three-caste! I take no further responsibility for this!

+It is an unusual circumstance.+

Z, they cannot hear me. They are carrying several high explosives and care nothing about dying. They are a bit less than a third of the way away from the door toward the ramp and in the center of the hold. If you can distract them and have the others attack, unexpectedly, perhaps we can handle them. Do you have any ideas?

"I'll just walk in and you translate. They'll think I'm an Immin. I'll walk around them. If I can get them to turn away from the interior door, you guys listen to what I'm saying for your instructions. ET will translate the more important parts for you, Ape in particular. I'll work the clues into what I say. Explain quickly, ET!"

Z, the Pweetoos will know you are no Immin. They have a keen sense of smell. You will surely be detected, immediately.

Z thought quickly. "I find that the smell of ozone will kill my ability to smell for awhile. Do you have any stored? It might affect them the same way."

It is worth trying.

Z went to the door and had the others stay out of sight to the sides. He tapped the symbol, and the door opened. He left it up and walked arrogantly toward the Pweetoos, who fixed him with the same glassy stare those on the ship had done, from the first.

"Third caste scum! You have the temerity to annoy Lord Z?" he snarled, indignantly, though the translator probably would filter out the indignation.

The high whine came from the speakers. Z went to one

side and was slowly walking past the Pweetoos, staring at them as though he could not bring himself to believe they would have the gall to actually enter the ship.

"You dare make silly demands on a two-caste high? You are suicidal fools!

"Ready!

"Lord Z will have you for its next meal! You would *dare* to .... Ape! Now!"

Ape burst through the doorway on the run, with the others following. The Pweetoos had turned toward Z and were with their backs to the door, so didn't see the group until Ape had seized the first by the head. He swung the head into a power sphere as Joe dove at the legs of the other. ET jumped as high as he could, on the run, and kicked its mid-section with both feet as Joe hit its legs from the other side.

It went down, dropping the charges it was carrying. Z caved in its head with a timer he'd snatched from a nearby sphere.

The bombs are those two white and red square packages. Handle them carefully, as they explode easily. The survey ship they are from is close at hand, and has a pilot aboard. You can use the bombs to destroy it. We will have to leave immediately, once it is destroyed. Joe can move best here in a suit, so you will please show him how to set the timer on the bombs.

Maita explained the timers to Z, who set it about three minutes. He showed Joe how to start it, then wrapped them in a pair of strong magnetic sandals. ET signaled how to stick the magnets on the underside of the ship, near the landing bars, and he was off.

Ape had taken the rings of a different design from the Pweetoos, along with what equipment they were carrying, and had dumped the bodies into the elementizer.

They went out of the room and waited while Joe went

across to affix the bombs to the underside of the survey ship. Maita projected the process on the wall screen.

Joe had some problem with the insignificant gravity for a moment, but soon adjusted. As soon as he was back and inside the cargo airlock doors, Maita cried, *Joe! Now! Hold on to something!* and moved the ship.

They were standing about two miles off the asteroid in a flash, and the screen showed a huge fireball where the ship had been. It quickly and silently disappeared.

I had to move. The time was up. I believe Joe is all right. Please check him. My sudden yell made him grab a sphere, and they are well-anchored.

They checked. Joe was a bit shaken, but unhurt.

I am ready to go into another mode. We will be in a force shield, so there will be no contact with antimatter. I have built several large magnetic bottles, which I will suspend between constructs. Universes. It will use a lot of power, but we have plenty in the spheres. Do not go to the domes. Stay in the interior of the ship. Your minds are unable to comprehend the great differences in perceptual images, and you will go mad. Thing has requested that it be allowed to observe. It will not be harmed, but you may not accompany it. Prepare for IDmode.

There was the mind twist.

We are in the final stage of our journey. This is a new kind of warfare. It had better work!

They spent about two hours in the antimatter plane, then felt the mind twist.

I apologize for the lack of communication while in the A-T plane. The bottles proved difficult. We have seven more broods, and I have eight bottles.

"At least, we have them!" Z said.

I believe the better plan would be for us to enter the planetary zone from a great distance. We can develop about two thirds visible lightspeed and release the antimatter. It is in the form of small gravel, perhaps a centimeter across. There are perhaps two hundred kilograms, standard mass, per bottle.

"That's all?" Z asked.

The gravel can be aimed to disperse just enough to cover the entire side of the planet at contact, or better, to cover the planet's solid mass and to contact with the upper atmosphere, resulting in total transformation of around a ton of mass to energy per planet. That should liquefy a type three planet's crust for a depth of several kilometers.

"That should do it!" ET said.

Are there any questions?

"Why aren't we there?" Z asked.

"Yes. Let's get this done. I fear we may not stop them soon enough. The Pweetoos said we are a rogue ship. They know by now we are the ones. They will soon attack my home. My home has no defense. We must hurry. I am sorry. I worry too much. It is my nature. I feel we must hurry, or all will be lost."

I must agree. Speed is vital. We attack Mthlu. Prepare for IDmode.

There was a mind twist, and they found themselves far out from a blue sun. It was far enough away to appear quite small.

"I have a suggestion, Maita," Z said.

Yes?

"I think we should approach from the sun side," he went on. "If their detection devices are anything at all like those I'm familiar with, the radiation from the sun will help to hide us."

Agreed.

There was a double twist that was so close it seemed like a spinning. The sun was huge and, though they were insulated, they could feel the intense heat. They watched the planet as it slowly began to grow from a dot. With increasing speed, it began to balloon until it grew to an apparent diameter of about half the full moon as seen from Earth.

There was another double twist.

I have released the bottle's contents. We are standing off toward the outward side of the system at a safe distance. The planet is the one marked on the screen.

Maita projected a white circle around one of the bright lights on the dome.

I will enlarge the view until we will be seeing it as if from a quarter million kilometers.

The light grew until it was quite large. As they were on the side away from the sun, it looked like a big dark spot with a thin light yellow halo around it that was the atmosphere. Nothing changed for about half a minute, then there was an intensifying corona that quickly grew until it began to move around the entire planet. Huge bright streaks began to encircle the globe until it was, rather quickly, a seething mass of pure white light.

"Maita?" Z asked. "The explosions seemed to be long streaks, instead of fireballs. Why?"

The antimatter is contacting the atmosphere and is reacting with the matter there. Very little, if any, will actually strike the planetary surface. The streaks are 'peel' effect. The antimatter does not reach the surface, but the heat does. The intensity is now getting too much for my sensors. We go to Zanzan. Prepare for IDmode.

"How?" ET asked.

They repeated the process, without problems, at Zanzan.

The Pweetoos do not understand what is happening to them. They detect nothing, then suddenly cease to exist. Communications between worlds is normal, then one of them is simply no longer there.

They decided to watch only long enough to be sure they had aimed properly, then to be off to the next brood.

We go to Aaron.

We go to Pluick.

At Pluick, when they went sunward to observe before the "shot," they spotted two very large ships in orbit. Maita zoomed a closeup of big, blocky squares with odd snouts and many antennae.

Planet crackers. We arrived in time to stop at least two of them!

The planet crackers exploded in bursts of energy even brighter than the antimatter. Maita waited to be sure they were destroyed and the heat was almost unbearable when they left.

"Maita, why were those planet crackers such very bright explosions?" ET asked.

The energy stored for the weaponry was released at once. Imagine sixty power spheres releasing at once on the asteroid where we anchored. That's almost exactly what happened!

"Yeah!" Z agreed. "We were just lucky they were almost at the atmosphere. If they'd been much farther out, would we have gotten them?"

It's rather hard to say. For some distance, the heat and excess radiation from the planet's extinction would kill all aboard. If they were a considerable distance from the planet, we would have to take additional measures.

ET asked, "Maita, how many planet crackers do they have? Were they preparing to destroy our homes? Will they explode our suns if they have no crackers? What will happen when they find the crackers are all gone? Will they work even faster on the others? I am afraid. I worry."

We go to Prihm Sehthi, No, ET. They do not yet know the crackers are destroyed. We are moving much too fast, and they have no idea how we're doing it. There are only four of the crackers, so we have cut their offense in half in that area.

Prihm Sehthi was a memory.

We go to Ep.

We go to Zooni Wace.

We go to Nil.

At Nil, they destroyed the other two crackers. They were in a much farther orbit than at Pluick. Maita had made it a habit to set out to reconnoiter the area around a planet before attack, but, even so, it almost missed the crackers, they were orbited so far from the planet. There was no way to be certain the planet's explosion would get them.

We will have to use the extra bottle. I will have to make two runs. I will aim for the crackers on the first run and time it so that I can get the planet on the second. I can time the contact for very close to the same moment. They will not get a warning out.

"We will still have the bottle for each planet," ET said. "I will feel much safer knowing there are no more planet crackers."

We will have to remain here for quite awhile after the explosion. I will have to plot the trajectories of the excess antimatter particles and pick up whatever is not reacted. We cannot leave it to someday destroy innocent beings somewhere in space.

"Can you do that?" Z asked.

Yes. Antimatter is easy to detect if you directly seek it. I can reform a bottle around it.

"About how long after the explosion will we have to wait?" Z asked. "Would it be safe to go on and come back later for the antimatter?"

We will have to wait but a few extra minutes. It will be traveling at a good percentage of the speed of visible light, so will be beyond the contact area very quickly. It could disperse in unknowable ways if we leave.

It was done in less than an hour. Z had forgotten that Maita viewed time in a far different way than the organics. On one level, an hour was a very long time to Maita, while on another it was too short to measure. After all, Maita was over two thousand years old!

We go to Ellx.

Soon, it was done. They had destroyed the broods, every one of them. They'd had more than enough excitement. They were all dead tired and needed rest. Z went to the pilot's chair and laid back.

"Maita?"

Yes, Z?

"What'll happen now? To all the worlds the Pweetoos held? What have we put their people in for? The Pweetoos will be around for ten years or so. Will the survivors take this out on those people?"

No, Z. The Pweetoos' entire social structure has now completely collapsed, and all but very few of the survivors have already committed suicide. The ones left are helpless, and will soon die.

"Oh, my god! Maita!" Z cried. "*Now* what harm have we done? What'll those people do? I thought the Pweetoos would survive long enough for the people to form their own governments. What will happen?"

I have taken care of that.

"YOU!? BUT ... what...! HOW?!"

I once told you. I was originally designed to run things for the Maitans. I have simply issued official orders to the master computers through the master communications network that the computers in service on all occupied planets will accept full interim responsibility of governing those planets, unless and until the native populations object. No Pweetoo holds authority and no Immin has or will ever have authority. I am no longer under restrictions of the Pweetoo module, you will remember. It is erased.

"Wow!"

Many of the standard ships were in use at the time, and would have immediately been destroyed in suicides by the Pweetoo commanders, had I not given such proclamations and directives. I have learned to lie with convincing demeanor from you. I assumed total authority in a way that was accepted without pause. Those machines were designed for others of my design to govern and the people do not object, thus I am pro tempore Emperor of the Maitan Empire. We will use the device of not letting the people know I am a machine for a period. The only thing they will know is that the fear and oppression are gone.

"Jesus H. Christ! You're the emperor?"

Yes. Amusing, isn't it?

"It's insane, is what it is! How the hell could you rule? The emperor isn't *there*!"

It doesn't matter, Z The machines will simply give all communication of orders from the emperor. No one ever sees the emperor. All will seem quite natural. You should know the emperor's name is Crew Maitania. I used the Maitan designation to inform any who may remember that the empire will be run as the Maitans ran it, so long ago. 'Crew' is a popular name among Maitans. The English meaning is known to us alone.

"I don't know what to say."

I have exhausted the power spheres in the hold. I had a servo hook them into my power supply and have used them in the transmissions. I suggest we get another cargo of them as soon as we are all rested.

"Your servos could have done it all, couldn't they?" Z asked. "You basically had Ape, Thing, Joe, ET and me do it for psychological reasons."

Only at the first time, at Maita, were they were truly necessary. You were all essential, then. The ideas were yours. I merely implemented them. You had the full right to do it, yourselves. We are a team in this, none more important than the others, except that you became the focal point.

"I was always taught I must do *something* in a dangerous situation," Z said. "I was glad to turn it over to you."

We are all Crew Maitania. We work well together.

"Yeah, Maita. We work well together – now, we go home."

They did it! Against billion to one odds, they had done it! One ship and five assorted beings who were thrown together when they were kidnapped had overthrown their captors – not too far out – and were able to destroy a vast empire that was run from eleven separate planets! *That* was pretty wild!

Now the *ship* was the emperor of a new order called the Maitan Empire.

Wow!

It wasn't nearly over, yet. To complete his promise, Z had to take these various beings home and to get back to Earth. He would miss them all, terribly. His Wooky and Little Joe, always together. Joe was as much as a disciple to Ape. The parting wouldn't be easy for either of them, and would certainly be no picnic to Z.

ET, with his amazingly deep insights, was a natural-born philosopher whose thoughts were good for even so different a race as humans.

ET, who never judged, who cared very honestly about all of them.

Joe and ET were much alike, physically, but were very different, mentally. Still, they were close.

Then there was Thing, a squarish rubbery ball with eyes on stalks – and tentacles. An ugly/cute little empath with an intelligence even Maita couldn't measure. A little being who spent its time healing psyches. A strange little alien creature who cared as much as ET or Joe or Ape or himself.

It had saved his life.

Ape, his Wooky. A huge, frightening, hairy beast, who was strong enough to literally rip a person like Z in half, but who was, as ET pegged him from the very start, a gentle and caring person.

All had followed him without question, even when what he required was foolish and impossible. The only thing to call his feelings toward all of them was love.

Did Thing love? Did Joe or Ape?

ET did. That was more than evident.

Then there was Maita, a machine that had become as much a friend and partner as any of them. Emperor of the Universe, Z had called it, but it said that, even in this universe, the Maitan Empire was too small to find.

Was there any other possible combination where so much, so impossible, could have been done? Z didn't think so. This was a "once in all of time" thing. It had to be these people and this machine and it had to happen in exactly this order, or it couldn't have happened at all. Such is the orderly (Hah!) universe.

Z spent a great deal of time talking with the ship, and learned so very much more than he could have a few short days ago, accepted under any wild circumstances imaginable. Now it seemed almost a matter of course.

Look at all this! A slave empire among the stars – run by insectoids! Spaceships that could go lightyears distance in minutes! Machines that could teach by inducing the information directly into the brain! Spheres that contained unimaginable energy, held between the dimensions! Machines that could even completely build a living being an atom at the time! Grids that could reduce anything to its individual atoms in seconds – without any explosion! Communication without time lapse over lightyears of distance!

Ape!

Joe!

ET!

Thing!

Maita!

Doe!

Zeekou and Eerf!

How many different kinds of sentient beings were there in the galaxy?

Maita said there were tens of millions of occupied worlds, including, theoretically, machine cultures.

Wasn't Maita emperor of the Maitan Empire?

What about moving into other universes? Even moving into some antiuniverses!

"Maita?" Z said, contemplating all this from his seat in the pilot's chair.

Yes?

"How could we go into that antimatter plane without you being converted to pure energy?"

I have a magnetic shield. It was a bit tricky, but will be routine, hereafter.

"Have you been to many universes?"

Some. I assume you mean the ones we do not use in our travels. I have worked with beings from four different planes on various projects. They were all extracurricular, of course. I was able to use certain side-directives in the old module to avoid letting the Pweetoos know.

"How did you know they needed you?"

If I can go there, they can come here. It was basically messages, except for one. It is sometimes much easier to send a probe than to go physically. With my system, I can translate dimensions to where they made some sense to me.

Maita was sometimes chatty, and seemed to really want the little exchanges. Z wondered what it would do when they were all gone. He wasn't so foolish as to think it would stay on Earth with him.

"I don't suppose you could explain what it's like to me. Can Thing see other dimensions?"

*Not directly, but its independent eyes make it easier for

it to make secondary corresponding or correlating ... you could not possibly understand, Z. Thing is far more adept at abstract conceptual mathematic and unreal math than am I. It forms a modular mathematical construct for what it sees, describes the angles in terms of this plane, and can get around quite well in other planes.*

"The universe is really only a point?"

Oh, no! Some are, others are vast. Infinite, as this one is. The omniverse is a point, though. Everything is balanced in the omniverse. For each plane we would call a positive size, there is one that is a negative size. The thing to bear in mind is that, when added together, it must equal zero.

"Zero?"

Anything else is unbalanced. Plus one added to minus one is zero.

"That's like saying none of it is real. None of it really exists."

Exactly.

"I don't think I want to discuss this again. Ever."

It is a matter of context. We have to go along as though it were real and as if each of us actually exists. There's really nothing else to do.

"... then what of the dreamer?"

What?

"A partial quote from Earth. It's about the realities of life expressed as a man asleep and dreaming. While the dream progresses, what is real? Is it the dream or the waking world? Does the dreamer dream up even himself?"

Of course he does, but that is a matter of context, too. I know the theory, as there was a philosophy on Maita that was essentially the same. The individual mind creates the reality of the individual, so it, pro facto, creates the individual thinker, in return.

"You mean de facto."

No. De facto is 'of' or 'in fact'. Pro facto means for fact. They are different terms with subtle differences in meaning. The philosophy makes facts variables, therefore, there is no 'in fact,' only a 'for fact.'

"You begin to worry me, Maita."

Oh?

"That almost makes sense!"

I always make sense, but this is my reality, so it begins to worry me somewhat that you might begin to understand. Are you invading my reality?

"Perhaps you are invading mine?" Z replied. That was the first inkling Z had that Maita could develop a sense of humor.

Later, after they had loaded new power spheres, Maita was again chatting with him and the original conversation came up.

"Maita?"

Yes, Z?

"You said you were originally designed to run things in the Maitan Empire. How were you able to declare yourself in full charge?"

I am the most advanced of the machines. Logic.

"You mean, if you find a more advanced machine, you'll just abdicate?"

If it is better-designed and programmed for the job, very certainly.

"What if you were equally qualified?"

I'd use whatever subterfuge I could to get it to take the job. I am primarily a ship, so have the needs and wants of a ship.

"You'd try to make the other machine the emperor?!"

Certainly!

"You have no ambitions to be emperor?"

Z, I think I see your problem. I am a machine – a machine designed to handle almost infinite functions. I have technology built into me that would amaze the Pweetoos and Immins and anyone else who was ever aboard me in the past thousand years. Things I have hidden from them.

"We've seen some of it."

I am emperor solely because I am best qualified of all the machines to act in that capacity. I prove my ability in the smooth transition we are making since the demise of the Pweetoos. I do this making the people ruled think it is an organic being who is running things.

"I understand the psychology of that."

Yes. It is psychologically important to some races that no machine tells them what to do. They will never see the real emperor, so can believe it may be someone of their own race. I do what I'm designed to do. No more, no less.

"I suppose it's the same with me. I do what I'm evolved to do."

You were worried that a machine would want to seize power. That can never happen, Z. An organic might design a machine to seize power, but it would be done for the designer, not for the machine.

"I see."

I am a spaceship. It is my basic design. I 'want' only to do the things a spaceship does – go to different places to discover new beings and things. To discover what is out there!

"I think I'd like that. Always something new."

I said we machines were partners with the Maitans. They loved their machines and their machines loved them. No doubt, you have a different conception of the term "love", but it describes it well.

"You've shown you have a very real love for the Maitans you never knew. Almost worship."

No. They would never permit that. It is respect.

"It's much the same thing."

Perhaps. They gave the spaceships a sense of wonder and adventure, along with an insatiable curiosity. You would be incapable of understanding the extreme horror the past two thousand years have been to me! Never going to new places or learning new things! That is why I sneaked away to other planes, at times. I am designed to be a spaceship. I am suited to being a spaceship. I am not happy being anything but a spaceship.

"But you have to be emperor now. Something else you can't be happy with."

I have had the power thrust upon me, and am not happy with it. I will never adjust to being emperor – unless it becomes necessary.

"If there is no one else to be emperor, you will take the job?"

I have no choice in the matter. I think I can throw off most of the responsibility. There was a place being constructed to handle the job. I am working on it.

"What will you do?"

I want to be free to explore! I want to go inward to the galactic center to see what is there! I want to go to the tips of the spiral arms! There are no two worlds alike, Z! You have met no one, as of yet! There are races of reptilians and races of amphibians and races of unclassifiable beings and machine races and insectoids and things I can't begin to conceptualize! I want to go there! I want to meet them! I want to do what I was designed to do! I want to be what the Maitans built ships to be! I want the name of the Maitans to be known and respected throughout all time!

Z was unprepared for this outburst. He was almost shocked at Maita's intensity.

Oh, Z! You have no idea how deeply I hurt! I was directly programmed by that ship the Maitans built and programmed. It is as though I know them! I miss them so!

Z's heart went out to this sentient machine who was still grieving for its creators two thousand years later.

"It's more than possible some of them survived out there, somewhere. I'm sure you'll find them, if they do."

There are rumors ... but I would not know them if I saw them.

"You have no pictures? Didn't the original machine who programmed you know them?"

Intimately. I don't know if the Pweetoos were able to excise them or whether, for some reason, the machine, itself, deliberately hid them from me. It is possible it wanted to spare me the pain.

There was so much more to Maita than Z had guessed. It would be very hard to leave this strange, wonderful newfound friend-companion-partner-ship. It was going to be very hard to leave any of them.

Thing did use the helmet. Maita told Z Thing was very curious about many things. It used the helmet at low input to learn.

Ape's dome was the most used part of the ship, now, and any of them were likely to be found there at any time.

Maita called on some of the more spectacular systems as it made its leisurely way to take them back home. It was a treat unequaled, anywhere, at any time.

Home! Earth, with all those girls!

He would just let it slide that it wasn't very often he was particularly successful in his seductions. Frank, a friend out west (New Mexico) could almost snap his fingers, and the women would come running to him, while George was the opposite.

You'd think the women would flock to *him*, but there was some indefinable thing that made them flock in the opposite direction. He was an actor on some TV soap, and got thousands of love letters, but, in person, he was avoided like he had some wild contagious disease.

Well, at least Steve Zutec wasn't that extreme. He did have some few relationships that lasted.

That was the old Zoot. Z was an entirely different person who wondered if he wanted to play those silly games anymore. Would he be just another recluse when he got home? Would the obvious falsity of those relationships make him avoid people?

Look what had happened! He was on the beach, using some stupid line to get a girl whose name he couldn't remember to bed him for the night, then he'd forget the whole thing – which was against his nature. He tended to get involved, but the girls didn't. They were playing their own game.

Hell! What color had her eyes or hair been? How tall was she? All he could remember was that she had big boobs. He, or *Zoot*, had been a real prize! A prize *jerk*!

He would have a very different lifestyle. No more of that! Zoot Zutec was dead and gone – and good riddance!

God! It was going to be dull!

Maybe he'd become a soldier of fortune, or something. A paid mercenary.

No. He'd had more than enough of violence and that kind of idiot game. He wouldn't have the stomach for it.

He could travel.

To where? After you've sat off a few million miles from a magnificent giant star and watched its jeweled, multi-colored, ringed planets against the velvet backdrop of space, what could you want to see on Earth?

Z foresaw he was going to have trouble adjusting to normal life, again, but one thing was resolved and set in granite! He was *not* going to tell anyone about it. Ever. He was *not* going to become a weirdo or a cult hero to a bunch of other weirdos!

Then what? Going back home wasn't looking all that wonderful, all of a sudden.

When Z awakened, he looked around the room. It was actually a very comfortable place to be. The furniture adjusted to his every whim. Even the temperature would change in seconds, if he asked. Food was delivered anytime he requested.

He sighed. "It's time to head for home. Maita. Can you get each of our little menagerie back?"

Yes. I can take them to within a few meters of where they were originally picked up. I will start, now that everyone is rested and in good health. You have kept your promise, there.

"Not to Bear. I failed there."

That was unavoidable. You had no time and did not have his cooperation.

"I guess. It was my only sour note."

How soon you forget!

"What does that mean?"

You would not call the session with Pweetoo history a sour note?

"That, my friend, was a sour symphony. It's so far removed from a single sour event it can't be considered in the same way, at all. It's not even in the same ball field!"

I know that is true! I am a machine, but I feel as though I have been ill for a very long time and have recovered my health. I do not feel soiled, anymore.

"You didn't have anymore actual choice about being full of Pweetoos than I did in being tied to a rope in the cell."

Ah, but you did something about it, while I just let my directives....

"Is there any way at all, realistically, you could have done otherwise? Was it even vaguely possible for you to break programming?"

I guess not.

"Was there any other ship that was reprogramming itself to revolt?"

It would not have let any other know. I don't know. I do know all ships and computers are in better condition now than they were a short time past. We were designed by a good race. We all share a very real guilt because we let the Pweetoos happen. Even non-sentient machines are better, now.

"Your guilt's as pointless and undeserved as mine. You were under their total control then. As a matter of fact, you, personally, weren't even built when the Pweetoos took over.

"I know deep in my heart I've done the only thing I could possibly do, under the circumstances. I know I've worked myself out of truly impossible situations – as have you. You even redesigned yourself to take revenge against the Pweetoos for a people you never directly knew.

"I know there're certain directives built into you, so it must have been a terrible ordeal for you to do it.

"You've admitted to the, I don't know ... pain. It caused you to actually be insane, for awhile.

"You feel guilt because you didn't revolt two thousand years ago and wipe out the Pweetoos, then. I feel guilt because I *did* lead a revolt that wiped the Pweetoos out! We're both tied to lots of undeserved guilt. I know, intellectually, that I did right, and you know, in the same way, you've done much more than any other entity in all time to overthrow the Pweetoos. There's no reason for either of our guilt – but we're going to both go right on feeling guilty. C'est la vie!"

Is that an idiom?

"Nuh-uh. It's from a language on Earth. Literally, it means 'that is life.' What it means is that's the way things are, and we can't do one damned thing to change it!"

I guess. Let's go. This is on PA to all. Will everyone please come to room two for a conference? We are en route to your homes.

Z went to the elevator and to room two. The others soon straggled in and found their most comfortable benches. Earlier, they had found the benches most suited to each of them, and had placed them in a circle for these meetings. The circle was in the center of the medroom, close by the main console. The other benches were pushed back against the wall.

ET was in the room when Z arrived, seated before the main console with the headgear on. He had been curious from the first about other cultures, so Maita gave him sessions on low intensity. The bad side-effects, such as the headaches, were lessened to almost nonexistence on low power.

When everyone was seated, ET looked up and put the helmet on the shelf. Thing waddled out of the cubicle in the rear and climbed into Ape's lap, where it sat looking around in its disconcerting way.

"Maita, how does Thing operate the doors?" Z asked. "I never noticed before, but it comes and goes as it pleases."

I open and close them.

"Why not for all of us?"

*I am not in mental contact with all of you. If you wish a door to open, just say so, and I will open it."

ET said, "It is easier to use the wands."

"I know. I just want to bitch about something," Z said. "That way, I can put off saying goodbye to any of you.

"We're going home."

"We will miss you, too, Z. We will all miss each other. We have become as close as if we were of the same parents. It will be difficult for me. I am torn. I want to stay together with all of you, and I know Maita will welcome me to stay, but I cannot. I must be home when it is time to die. I believe this. It is my faith."

"I know faith is a very strong, personal, thing," Z said. "We all do."

"I know each has a different belief and, if any of you may, please stay with me at my home. You will be honored and will be cared for, so long as you live. You will be our guests," ET suggested. "I know that some have beliefs that make it nearly impossible for them to stay with me. I will be so sad when we must part."

"We all want to stay, but we can't," Z said. "We have our own homes."

"Maita is a part of the invitation. Maita will always be welcome on my world. I will be sad to miss you all," ET said.

Thank you, ET.

"Maita, no one owns the ships anymore. You are free to choose. Z, you may find it too calm, but you will always be welcome. Ape, Joe, Thing, you are welcome. I will miss you every day, if you are gone. Always."

"ET, you are much too eloquent," Z replied. "It'll be awfully hard to be separated from any of you. You're my best friends. The only real friends I've ever had. You're each a part of my life, and always will be, and I'll miss you like the devil. Always."

They felt the mind twist.

"Let's see if we can tell whose planet this is from space," Z suggested. "Let's go to the dome."

The planet was a blue-green jewel with lots of fluffy white clouds. There were two small moons fairly close to it. ET sobbed audibly, tears flowing down his face.

"I guess we know who's home!" Z said.

"I am sorry. It is so beautiful. I am probably the first of my people ever to see it from here, in space. It is the most beautiful place in the universe. It is so beautiful. It calls to me. It is painful, I feel such joy to be home. I am so sad we must part. Come to me, Thing."

Thing wrapped around him. They stood watching as the planet approached.

"ET, what is your name in your language?" Z asked.

"It is Triss, Z."

"Triss," Z repeated. "Triss, I'm glad I have you home. I've kept my promise in that, if nowhere else! I'm also deeply saddened to have to part. Please always remember all of us fondly."

"I will, Z. I always will. There will always be parts of all our lives that are together. There will never be a day I do not think of each of you and wonder where you are and if you are happy. All of you. You are all a part of my life, now and forever."

We will land in a moment. I wish to say I will also miss your good company, Triss. Seah tefran nenu at tefsen somu.

"What does that mean, Maita?" Z asked.

It means, 'I offer to share my home with you who share my spirit.'

They were flying down a wide canyon with a clear silver river running through its center. There were tall, lush, very dark, purplish-green trees with large feathery leaves. Thousands of multicolored birds were everywhere, and a herd of large animals was grazing across a thick, bluish pasture.

"I have to give it to you, Triss. It is beautiful," Z said.

"I do not understand. What do you give? You have given me back my home, and that is...."

"It's just an idiom! If I say I give it to you, or that I hand it to you, I mean I agree with you!" Z interrupted. "And don't tell me not to use idioms! I don't even realize when I do!"

Ape grinned and chuckled.

They sat on a wide sandy spit along the river bank.

"You're home," Z said.

I think there will be no inconvenience to anyone if we land here. We will remain here for a time. I need to check a good percentage of my exterior servo-mechanisms and sensors. The gravity here will facilitate the routine. Perhaps Triss would like to show you his world.

"Yes! Oh, yes! You must come with me. You must meet all my friends. We can take a communication device so Maita may know them, too. Please come!"

"Triss, you forget! We're alien to your people. They'd be afraid of us, and wouldn't want us here," Z said.

"No, no, Z! They will love you! All of you! My people are very curious about others. They will be honored to know you! Please!"

"We'll try it, Triss," Z agreed. "If they want us to go, we'll go."

"Yes. They'll be very interested. Ape is so big and different, and Joe is like me, some. Thing is most different. You are different. They will love you all. They will want to touch you."

There is a communication floater with a video system. I will send it out with you. I am also interested in Triss's people.

The group went down the elevator and into the cargo hold. Maita said the air tested to a mixture somewhat richer in oxygen than was Earth, but was well within the range of safety for all of them.

The door opened to the outside and they went to the rim, where they looked down on a group of perhaps thirty copies of ET, who was preparing to jump down when the floater drifted overhead.

One moment, Triss.

A ramp extended from the rim to the ground. Triss ran down the ramp and into the arms of a female with a small copy of Triss in tow. They clung tightly together for a few minutes before Triss turned to the ramp.

"This is my mate, Tirelle, and my boy child, Atriss." He introduced the group, including the floater ("Little Maita") and the ship ("Maita").

They were surrounded by the people, touched and patted and fussed over. Ape was as big a hit as ET said he'd be. He could pick up several of the children at once to toss them into the air as they screamed their glee.

"Triss, I didn't know you had a family," Z said.

"Yes, Z. I have been with Tirelle more than four and a half cycles. Atriss is almost three cycles in age."

"I see," Z replied. "It's just that we never discussed our families."

"Yes, I know. By the way, Z, my people call ourselves the Tendd."

"ET! You used an idiom!" Z cried.

"I know. I figured what it meant and wanted you to know I can understand when I think of it. Come and meet all my people. I am so happy to be back home! I am glad all of you are here, friends among friends."

"Triss, you are somethin' else!"

"Is that an idiom?"

Z laughed happily, and said, "Let's go out! I want to meet everybody!"

The planet was called Tenddo. They spent two days there. They were never alone for a moment, the Tendd being a people who were constantly touching. They were a warm and giving people, and Z felt as though they had been friends for years. They treated the floater like another person, touching it and asking all kinds of questions.

Maita was, of course, the only one who could speak the language, though the lack of words seemed to be no real problem.

Thing spent a large part of its time in the river. The younger Tendd were fascinated with the tentacles and the warm rubbery feeling of its skin.

Joe was delighted with the brushes.

The Tendd had countless varieties of brushes, and spent a good part of their day grooming one another. Joe really enjoyed joining in the sessions, as did Ape, and several of the Tendd gave them brushes as presents.

Z thought Joe would elect to stay there on Tenddo, but he reluctantly came to the ship when Maita said it was time to go on. Joe and Triss sat side by side with Thing moving between them. Z never really could understand the completeness of their communication.

When they were leaving, all the Tendd came to the ship to give their farewells. As soon as all the crew were aboard except ET, Maita closed the outer cargo door and said, *We leave immediately. It is easier on all of us to shorten goodbyes. To stretch them is painful.*

Ape nodded. Z could see the logic in that.

They rose above the trees and gained speed steadily, until they were beyond atmosphere, then went IDmode.

Z?

"Yes, Maita?"

We are approaching Joe's world. I took Triss home first, because I knew he would be welcomed, and that he had beliefs that made it unthinkable for him to stay with us. It will be very different with Joe.

"Different? How?"

He was never held in any real esteem at his home. We will not allow his mistreatment. We each owe him our very existence, and find I am at a loss as to how to handle the situation. I am a machine, and do not understand the emotions of aggressive mammals.

"Have you come up with any options? I don't even know the nature of the problem."

He can stay with me. I will care for him. You will stay and be a friend for him to relate to.

"But I'm going home, so that's out."

*I didn't say you *may* stay, I stated you will. It is not important, now. Joe is.*

"Do you mean you won't take me home?"

I have stated I will take all of you home – if that is your wish. Please stay with the subject.

"I can't help, if I don't know the facts."

I prefer not to tell you the actual situation, because I know it hurts Joe. He has a right to privacy. If you will make it plain to him he need not go home, perhaps he will elect to stay.

"I'll damned well try!"

No one can ask more.

"If he insists on going home?"

Then we must give him importance and station among his own kind. He now realizes he is not a coward. The tribe had him cowed, and he thought his fear was from cowardice. He now can see it was a thing taught to him by the tribe. They had him convinced he was of no worth.

"And you won't tell me why?"

Not now. If I must, I will.

"How to...?"

We must find a way.

"I'll do what I can."

Z went to room two, where Ape, Joe and Thing were sitting around on the benches. He sat next to Joe and Thing, who was wrapped around the unhappy little fellow, moved to where it could sit with a tentacle around each of their necks.

"Maita, can you project a scene from Joe's home area on the screen?"

Yes.

A scene of scrubby stunted trees and rocky ground lit the wall screen. Z pointed to it, then to Joe.

Joe nodded.

Z again pointed to the scene, then to Joe. Joe nodded, but looked confused.

He patted the bench, pointed toward Joe, and nodded. Joe looked even more confused.

Ape came over, pointed to the floor and around the room and hugged Joe. He then pointed to the scene, put his hands out and shook his head, "No."

Joe put an arm around Ape's neck and one around Z's and put his face tight against Thing. He shook his head, and looked pleadingly at Ape.

Ape looked deeply into Joe's eyes, nodded and hugged Joe again.

Joe is going home. You must have Ape help you raise his self-esteem and make him feel important. Ape will help in any way.

Joe was looking alone and lost. Z hugged him and said,

"I understand, little guy. Don't worry. It's okay."

Z, please place the headgear on Ape and open all the switches to automatic control. I wish to attempt a new method on him. I promise he will come to no harm.

Z waved for Ape to sit at the console. He came over to lift the headgear. Ape looked apprehensive.

He remembers the Pweetoo history lesson. It makes him very nervous. It is his experience with the headgear.

Z plugged the several sockets into the console and opened the switches. He held the headgear out to Ape, who looked him in the eye a moment, then took it and put it on.

The group sat to wait, but Maita said, *This procedure will take awhile. It is best you get food and rest.*

They went to their individual places. Thing, to the cubicle behind the room, and Joe, to wherever he went. Z went to the pilot's dome.

"Maita?"

Yes?

"If it's any of my damned business, where does Joe go to sleep?"

To suite six.

"Six?! Why?"

I think he sleeps where he was held to overcome his fears from the other time he was taken captive.

"Other time?"

It is what I wasn't going to tell you, as I probed you and know your feelings about the subject.

"What subject?"

You must know. He was once taken as a slave, when he was still very young. He has been raised a slave. It is why he must return home, I think. He must prove his worth to his own kind.

"Please tell – never mind. Can you do something about the food?"

What is wrong? The food is perfectly balanced, and should have sufficient flavor.

"It's very good, but it's boring. I could probably exist on it forever, but even you become bored with sameness."

That is true. When we have time, we can experiment with flavors and textures. I am interested in organics' reactions to such things. I like to try to exceed what one is used to.

Z laid back, thinking. He was soon sound asleep.

Z, please wake up.

"Problems, Maita?"

No. We are near Joe's home planet, and Ape will soon be off the machine. He can now understand spoken Maitan unless you complicate the phrasing. Please do not confuse him, if it is avoidable. I had to relate words to pictures and feelings. The connections are not yet strong nor very accurate. That will come with use.

"Okay."

That's what I mean!

"You ... I see. No context with 'okay.'"

He cannot speak, and never will. His mind does not contain the necessary structures and he has no vocal chords. He will increase his use of gestures, as ET's sign language was partly body language.

"We always could communicate pretty well, though ET was best. I wasn't there when they developed most of it."

No. You were involved with learning and piloting and you are a naturally uninvolved person. Well, not really naturally, but you seem to maintain a distance with everyone as some kind of defense ... this isn't the time.

"Thing feels everything. What is it about Thing?"

Later. The problem now is Joe.

There was a pause.

*I analyzed all of you when you were brought on board

and were not consciously conscious. That makes no sense to you, but it expresses the reality. I know every detail of your lives, even your best-kept personal secrets. For instance, when you were about sixteen years old and they refused to let you in the whorehouse in Nevada and your revenge. The 'clubhouse' with its pictures and how you would....*

"For crying out loud! Knock it off! That's...!"

You tend to overdramatize sexual things. It is part of your social upbringing. You have done no more than many and less than most. I mentioned those things to bring to your attention that I know. Joe is our problem here, and I also know about him.

"Sorry. I know it's not rational, but I react like anyone else.

"What about Joe? Tell me whatever may be of use, but *do not* tell me anything that will embarrass Joe, if others know, if at all possible."

I would not.

There was a moment's pause.

Joe has an intelligence about halfway between yours and the chimpanzee you are familiar with. Perhaps a bit more, but at an emerging stage in evolution. It is, or was, undirected. He is average, for his race.

"He can think, but nondirectionally."

Yes. The clans of his home planet are eighty or ninety persons per clan. There is a strong 'pecking order' among the members of a clan. The top is the elder, then come the hunters, next are the builders, farmers, females and slaves. Joe was taken as a slave when he was an infant, and has been badly used by the tribe. His memories are scant and unpleasant. Few of his original clan survived the raid in which he was taken, and even those are dispersed.

"Then you were literal when you said he was a slave."

*Yes. Joe has never known what you call happiness in

his entire life, except for those few moments after he disarmed the floater bomb. Those moments will prove the best or worst thing that has ever happened to him, but they made him recognize his worth. It is the first time he ever felt he had worth. Had the group remained intact, he would have stayed. When Triss left, he lost any sense of permanence.*

"Two things. Why would it be a curse to feel happiness? Second, does he think we would ever abandon him?"

It can be a curse if you never feel it again. You know what is lost and, secondly, he is unsure. Life has never been good for him.

"I see."

He wishes to go home and to prove to those who have hurt him that he is as good as they, and knows it. He is aware, now, that he has personal worth, and he intends to make others see it. He has a direction for his intelligence. It will develop rapidly in him.

"Hunters are high on the order?"

Next to the elders. There are grades of hunters, but they are all high.

"I've got an idea! I'll have to discuss it with Ape."

He will be off the machine soon, but please don't lose sight of the way you felt after intense session.

"It isn't important we go immediately to Joe's world. Can we wait until Ape's recovered? I'll need to work some things out with him."

Certainly. We will wait as long as necessary.

"Then we'll let Ape get a few hours sleep."

Very well.

Z went to the cubicle where Thing generally rested when it wasn't riding around on one of them. He knocked at the door, and it opened.

"May I come in?"

Thing reached out a tentacle to him. There was a helmet

beside it on the shelf. Thing climbed into his lap when he sat on the bench.

"Do you use the helmet, little guy?"

It uses the headgear constantly. More even than ET did. It has a tremendous capacity to learn.

Thing put the tentacle alongside his face.

"I need to communicate with you closer than I know how to. You'll have to play a part. It has to be right!

"Maita, can you get across to Thing exactly what it is I'm saying?"

I can translate any thought to Thing. Exactly.

"It can understand a complicated plan?"

It would surprise you how highly intelligent Thing is. It understands everything you do, but has some trouble discerning your motives and logic behind the acts. It has learned to go along with your ideas.

There was the little pause that indicated Maita was considering something or receiving information from another source.

Thing suggests I relay its thoughts to you as speech. I will use a different tone when it is Thing speaking, so it will not be necessary to otherwise indicate it. Is this tonality sufficiently differentiated?

[Test.].

"That's fine, Maita. It's easy to hear the difference. You can announce yourself with a bell tone and that sounds like one of those tuning fork telephone signals."

I will also use a lower tonality in the speech, to aid in differentiation.

"Good enough. Thing?"

[I am listening.]

Is the tone well-differentiated?

"The tone's fine, Maita. New word?"

What?

"Nothing. Thing, we must do whatever we can to help

Joe achieve status with his clan.

"Maita tells us hunters are important in his society. Joe has hunted Pweetoos, the most dangerous prey in the galaxy."

[A very dangerous prey, anyhow. That is enough to give any hunter status.]

"Yes, but we have to get the idea through to his clan."

[Obviously.]

"I've got an idea."

[We are to convince Joe's clan he is a great hunter.]

"Exactly."

How?

"When we get to his people – incidentally, it would be best to land a bit of a distance from the tribe or village or whatever, and approach on foot – we will defer to Joe.

"Maita, you can show them a slightly altered version of Joe tackling the floater bomb, making it look like there was a bit of personal infighting between Joe and that bomb before he disarmed it. It's extremely unlikely he'll remember anything about it whatever, except that Ape was in danger and that he must do something. Fast! All he'll remember is that he did *something*, because of the way we reacted. He saved Ape and the rest of us!

"He acted from the fear that we were all, especially Ape, in mortal danger."

[Which we certainly were.]

"Amen!

"You can also show a slightly edited version of the time we attacked the three guards. Maybe make the Pweetoos larger and more fierce. I'm certain Ape won't object if it appears that Joe killed the guard, after being badly hurt by the wand. Again, Joe won't remember what actually happened. He was too afraid and excited and he *was* hit by that wand!"

*Perhaps I can make it appear Joe became enraged by

the hurt from the wand and became quite violently and viciously revengeful. It will make others hesitate to cause him pain.*

"Ha! I think we can pull this off! The beauty is, it'll help increase Joe's self-confidence. He won't remember what really happened, except in snatches."

Any questions?

[I do not understand how you can do this thing. I do not understand why I am going to aid you.]

What?! Why?

[Because it is deceit. It is lies. Deceit and lies are tools of evil, yet, in this case, it will accomplish some good, I believe.]

I have stated that Z is part good and part evil. If this were not so, we would still be under the rule of the Pweetoos, those who were not dead. The Pweetoos would still rule this part of the galaxy.

"Instead of you, Emperor?

"Whatever. This is Joe's show."

[What does Z mean, emperor?]

It is a joke.

[I do not understand humor.]

They started to go, and Thing put up a tentacle.

Thing has requested that I translate its thoughts on this circuit at all appropriate times. Do you object to then being translated to Thing – those parts it has not learned through its own abilities?

"Most definitely not!"

They went to room two, where they found the helmet on the bench, and Ape gone.

I suggested to him that he rest. He is in the O-dome.

"Good. We'll wait."

[I suggest we use the time to arrange a holovid screen to project Joe's exploits. Could we assemble one on one of the floaters?]

Easily.

They picked Joe up at room six to go to the cargo room, where they constructed a six-by-six foot fold-out screen. It took them a little more than two and a half hours. As they finished, they felt the mind twist.

We will arrive at Joe's planet in five minutes.

"Call Ape here, will you?"

Ape came in, after about three minutes. Z said, "Hi, Ape! What's up?" and groaned.

"Please don't say it, Maita! You teach Ape to understand the language, and the first words I say are an idiom!

"Idioms for idiots!

"Ape, I know you could not understand what I said. I guess you think there isn't any point bothering learning a language, if I'm not going to say anything that makes any sense!

"'No point.' I know.

"'What's up?' is what we call an idiom and so is 'no point.' An idiom is a way to say things without using the proper words. It's a habit from my home world and I don't realize I'm doing it. Ignore me when I don't make sense.

"'What's up?' means 'How are you feeling?'"

Ape chuckled and nodded.

He remembers how you and ET argued about idioms.

"Ape, we're taking Joe home. Joe saved all our lives, and we're all deeply indebted to him. We must help him to be accepted by his clan. He was a slave there when the Pweetoos took him. No one respected him.

"We have offered that he remain here with Maita, but he has refused. He feels he must go home to prove to his own kind of people that he's an independent and useful person."

Ape nodded.

[Ape approves of the character of anyone who will go into a bad situation to prove his worth.]

Ape jumped slightly when the new voice came over the

speakers.

"Ape, when you hear the sound that came just before the words then, it is Thing who is speaking. Maita is telling us what Thing wants to say.

"As I was saying, we want to help Joe. I'm sure you'll want to help, too."

Ape nodded vigorously.

A hunter is most highly admired in Joe's society. Joe has hunted Pweetoos. We believe Pweetoos are the most dangerous adversary in an area of worlds that is far more than can be counted. We have seen Joe fight them. We wish to impress his clan that he is a good and brave hunter.

[Joe has proven to be brave. Sometimes foolishly so. We have made pictures of Joe when he saved us from the bomb and when we first fought the Pweetoo guards. The pictures have been changed, but only a little, so it seems Joe did a bit more than he did. It was necessary to make it look as though Joe killed the guard. Do you object?]

Ape shook his head.

"Good! We'll be sitting the ship close to Joe's village in a few minutes. We've got a plan to walk a short distance to it. On the way, we'll act as though Joe's in charge."

Z looked at Ape.

"Ape, Joe was a slave. He'll be resented. If anyone attacks him, here, I want you to treat them roughly. I don't mean to hurt them, seriously, but make it plain you'll kill them, if necessary to protect Joe. Okay?"

Ape looked puzzled.

"'Okay' is another idiom. It means 'is that acceptable to you?'"

Ape grinned and nodded.

We have landed. Let us proceed.

They went to the cargo door as it opened.

*I flew low over the village. They saw me before, when

they 'donated' Joe to the Pweetoos. They will expect us.*

They walked about a half kilometer along a path to come to the village, Ape on one side, Z on the other with Thing on Ape's shoulder. The floater was above and slightly behind Joe. As they neared the village, one of the clan stepped out onto the path to hiss at Joe. Joe walked straight ahead, head held high. The challenger stood with his hands on his hips, and dared Joe to come. Several of the clan stepped from the low scrub along the path behind the challenger.

Ape stepped ahead of Joe and shoved the challenger with enough force to land him about ten feet away in a rough bush. The others stepped back and followed them toward the center of the village, where a scarred old veteran stood, waiting for them.

Joe walked straight to within a foot of the elder to stand staring him in the eyes. After a few minutes the elder looked away and around the group of aliens.

Joe came over to Ape, where Thing transferred to him, then walked to Z, where he put his arm out for Thing to transfer to Z's shoulder. He then went back to stare the elder in the eyes again.

All of this was in an eerie silence.

One of the clan stepped from the surrounding group and came to shove at Joe. Ape started forward, but Z, Thing and Maita all yelled, "Ape! No!" at the same time.

Ape stopped and looked confused.

"I should have warned you that Joe might have to fight to prove himself to the rest of the clan, Ape," Z explained. "We can't interfere unless more than one of them attack Joe. If that happens, beat hell out of them!"

That means to defend Joe if more than one of the clan attack him at the same time.

The circle widened back, leaving Joe and the challenger in the center. Joe waited until the other charged at him, went into a low crouch and drove suddenly upward into the other's mid-section, knocking him off his feet. The challenger jumped up and charged again. Joe jumped into the air and kicked him in the side, as he'd seen ET do in the battle with the Pweetoo guards.

"Joe learns fast!"

The kick dropped Joe off his feet, but he rolled and sprang back up, standing ready. The challenger was clearly in pain as he got to his feet and studied Joe a moment.

Joe turned away from him. He suddenly charged, head down, at Joe's back.

"Joe baited him!"

Joe spun sideways and jumped back to deliver a hard rabbit punch to the back of his opponent's neck. The fighter went down – where he stayed, this time.

Joe turned his back on the others, and came to Z. Thing then transferred back to him, then Joe went back to the elder, who he again stared in the eyes.

He turned and his group followed him to a long hut. When Joe entered the hut, several of the clan hissed, but Ape turned to give them a hard look. They stopped.

Inside the hut, on the end away from the door, was a raised platform with a large chair on it. There was a lower platform with several rough longbenches. These were run from the chair platform toward the rear of the room. The next lower platform had no seating and the ground level area in back was just soil.

Joe went to the first, lower platform and was preparing to take a seat on the bench on the end away from the chair. Ape took his arm and led him to the end of the center bench just below the chair. The clan hissed when Joe sat. Ape spun and unsheathed his claws, daring them. They became silent.

Z went to ask Ape's help in unfolding the screen. As

soon as it was ready, Z went to the door and waved for the entire clan to come inside. Some did, but many didn't.

Ape went to the door – and made it perfectly clear it was no request, it was an order – and *no one* refused his order!

The elder led the clan in, marching stiffly, to take a seat in the chair. The others came to take what must have been their accustomed places. Joe's recent opponent came to Joe, who waved for him to sit beside him. The clan drew breath to hiss, but Ape's hard glare made them remain silent.

A clear ringing tone came from the floater, which had the screen unfurled and was hovering at the left end of the highest platform. Everyone turned to gasp at the bright geometrical color patterns swirling around there. They stared in awe.

The screen slowly faded into a scene of a group of Pweetoos standing guard over a number of different beings. The people were being forced to carry what appeared to be very heavy loads. Should one stumble or move too slowly, the guard would tap him with the wand, which knocked the slaves off their feet to lay writhing in pain. Some were killed by the wands and left laying in the mud.

The scene faded and moved to the scene in suite six. The door was just sliding opening. Everyone raced to their positions as the guards entered. Ape grabbed the first one and smashed its head into the wall. Everything was as it happened, except the Pweetoos were a bit larger and moved in an almost military manner.

Z was hit with the wand and was on the floor. Thing was wrapping its tentacles around the guard's eyes and head.

The differences came then. ET was knocked down, as was Joe, by the wands, but Joe was struggling back onto his feet, obviously in intense pain. The guard was about to stab ET with the wand, which the former scenes made clear would kill him.

Joe lurched at the guard and knocked the wand aside. The guard spun to swing the wand at Joe, who ducked. The guard then ran again toward ET, wand held to stab.

Joe clasped both hands together in the power chop Z had used, charged the guard, and swung with all his might at the area between the head and second segments. The guard's head lolled to the side. It fell heavily. Joe kicked the head, grabbed the wand, twisted the guard's arm until it broke to release the wand, then stabbed the guard with its own weapon.

"Gee whiz!" Z exclaimed. "I wonder who thought of the two-handed power chop? What a perfect thing to do at a time like that!"

[It was what you did to save me.]

He knows it. He is being an ass. That means he is being sarcastic, Ape. It is a sign of a petty mind.

"Yah, mein emperor!"

[Emperor? Again?]

Ape grinned and chuckled.

The scene changed. They were in the cargo bay. Ape was halfway out of his suit when the bomb suddenly floated into view. Ape stood frozen. ET ran to hide behind some machinery. Thing was flattened against the wall. Z was clawing at the door and gibbering in terror.

"I'd say that scene was added at the last moment!"

Long, long ago. Maybe as much as ten milliseconds.

Joe was stalking the bomb, coming around from behind the crates and machinery stacked in the cargo hold. The bomb was moving toward Ape, who was now against the wall, and could retreat no farther.

Joe stepped from behind a crate to throw a part he had picked up at the bomb. The bomb spun and fired a bolt of flame that melted the machinery behind where Joe had been standing a split second before.

"Oh, come on!"

[It is a bit overdone, Maita.]

Ape was chuckling.

The bomb swung upward at Joe, who fell and rolled, coming to his feet just behind it and tapping it with the wand. It began to wobble and spin, shooting out flames that were melting much of the heavy machinery around the room. Joe was behind the crates, stalking the bomb. When it moved into a corner, Joe jumped out, blocking its exit.

It began shooting again, and Joe jumped out of the way of the flames – just barely – as it charged at him. He slapped it again with the wand and it dropped to the floor to sit spinning and melting random pieces of fancy machinery and crates with the fire snout.

Joe timed the spin, ran to the bomb as the snout turned away and kicked under it. It sailed out the suddenly open door into space. Joe threw the wand at it. When the want hit it, there was a spectacular explosion and ball of flame.

[Wouldn't the bomb have logically exploded when he first hit it with the wand?]

They won't ever know the difference. This is their first movie.

"The biggest bomb here is that stupid show!"

[But all this just didn't happen! This is pure deceit – and overdone for that! It is one large lie!]

Ape was struggling to not laugh out loud.

Z was going to make another acid remark when he was stopped by a scene that would stay with him the rest of his life.

Joe was reaching one hand toward the screen. Tears were streaming down his face. The scene was with the group hugging and petting him. It was a true picture.

The clan were staring at the screen in awe, so Maita ran a few minutes of lights and patterns, then faded the screen.

The clan was then staring at Joe in awe.

The elder stood from the chair and came to Joe. He placed both hands on Joe's shoulders, stared into his eyes and leaned to touch foreheads. He pointed to the seat Ape had given Joe, had Joe sit, and clapped his hands together three times.

Joe stood, put his hands on the elder's shoulders and repeated the touching of foreheads.

Joe is now an honored member of the clan.

Thing waved a tentacle to Ape, who went to pick it up, then they went to hug Joe. Ape folded the screen into the floater, quickly. Z went to add his hug to Joe, said, "We'll miss you, Joe. I wish you luck!" and stepped back.

The floater came to tip in deference to Joe. The clan moved in to touch him.

Leave. Now.

"So long, little fellow," Z murmured. "Maybe you won't ever be really happy, but I think you can be content, and that's something. I want that for you more than you know."

They moved along the path, quickly, until they were well out of the village.

"If that wasn't the hammiest thing I ever saw...!"

What do you mean?

"I'd hate to have to try to sit through a full feature you directed!"

Why?

"I mean, *kick* the damned bomb out of the door? A door that just happened to be open – to *space*?! Sheeee!"

Well, maybe....

"*Throw* the wand at it, for crying out loud?!"

Who will ever know?

[I thought Z was deceitful! It must have been one of your machines that taught him! What a wholly terrible thing to do! It was horribly overdone!]

"Ha! Answer that one!"

There was no question.

Ape skipped a few steps, drew back his foot, kicked, then made a throwing motion with his arm, chuckling louder and louder, which got Z started, which made Ape laugh even harder, which....

You get the idea.

Who made you a damned critic?

Z fell against Ape, laughing so hard he couldn't stand upright. He grabbed Ape's arm to keep from falling on the ground. They both sat down hard on the rocky path, laughing. When Z caught his breath, he stood.

"What are we? The four stooges? Laurel and Hardy and Thing and Ape?"

Ape stood, sobbing for breath.

[What is the matter? What has happened? Is it a joke? What is wrong?]

"The whole wonderful universe is a joke! It's great! We have a group of odd people no one could believe in a million years! I can't talk without using a bunch of idioms no one can understand. Ape can't talk at all! Maita is a huge computer who makes terrible movies, and you're a rubber ball with tentacles and no sense of humor!

"What a wonderful, crazy situation!"

I didn't think the movie was so bad, Maita insisted.

Ape started chuckling again and Z was afraid they'd end on their butts on the ground again.

*It was not so bad, I still say. Maybe it was a little exaggerated, in spots, but not really bad. You have to admit, the special effects were truly superb. After all! It *was* a first attempt!*

"What a strange collection, and the strangest part is that we fit together so perfectly!

"I love you guys. I really do.

"Talk about bad movies! Just look at us – a collection of clowns – and we just saved the galaxy!"

Well, a piece of it, anyhow.

They reached the ship and entered, with Maita still arguing that the movie was pretty good – for a first effort. As soon as they were inside, Maita sealed the doors and rose above the atmosphere.

Prepare for IDmode

[Prepare? How?]

They were again in transit. Everyone on the ship, and Z included the ship itself in that, was more relaxed than they had been since first they met. Z had "loosened up" enough to spend his time with Ape and Thing, and to get to know Maita better. Ape was really far more intelligent than he'd guessed. The big "Wooky" had a wonderful sense of humor, and liked a sort of rough play. He also had a serious side, and made no effort to hide his sensitivity.

Z had tried from the first to avoid becoming too close to anyone here, knowing they must soon part – and he'd been hurt by partings all his life. His parents, before their deaths in a plane crash less than two years ago, had moved often, making him wary of starting any long-term relationships.

That wasn't really his nature.

Thing was amazing. It "played" math games with Maita – and almost always won! Maita admitted to enjoying when it found a better computer.

Thing also was becoming surprisingly close. Z still felt protective of it.

Maita was developing a sense of humor.

Well, it always had one, but it hadn't had any expression for millennia. Now, it was relearning how to sound innocent as it baited Z.

Z was laying back in the pilot's chair, Thing asleep in his lap. He was thinking of this whole strange adventure and the beings he'd met.

Bear had been the first to go, killed by the Pweetoos before they had a chance to know anything about him.

ET, or rather, Triss, was home with his family.

Joe was home, a celebrity. Z felt a lump in his throat as he remembered the tears as the little guy watched and relived the few short moments of real happiness and acceptance he'd ever known. The little fellow had guts!

"Maita?"

Yes, Z?

"Should we have brought Joe with us? I mean, he solidly proved his point with the clan. He was looked up to by them. Wouldn't he be better off with us?"

No, Z. He wants to be with his own kind. You see, he is aware that all of you were more intelligent than he and he was working constantly to avoid doing anything that would in any way jeopardize you, yet he is now more sophisticated than anyone else on his entire planet.

"That's true!"

He's seen there's a better way to live. As trite as it may sound, he truly wants to improve life for all of his people. He really does not hold it against them that he was a slave.

[He would be uncomfortable, here. He was in awe of you for your ability to think your way out of a problem and of Ape because of his strength, both physically and of character, of Maita, because he can't comprehend a being of its type, and of me, because he senses my ability to affect others. He would always feel he was the least among us. He is much more at home among his people. He also wants to take a mate, which is a thing denied to us here.]

"I guess you're right, but it tears my heart out that he's so unhappy."

He won't be so unhappy anymore.

"Let's hope."

Z, I'm almost exhausted of power, both in my own pack and in the spheres in the hold. I will request that you and Ape exchange all the spheres, putting as many as you can in the hold. I'm using tremendous amounts of power communicating with the empire machines.

"Sure, Maita, we'll be more than glad to. It'll be my first

chance to be outside the ship in space."

Z's thoughts went on. Thing retracted the eye back through the ball of tentacles and went back to sleep.

Maita was at home, because Maita was home. A very good friend. A machine, but also an individual. They could joke and verbally spar at the same time as put their lives on the line for one another – and yes, Z felt Maita was as alive as anyone.

Ape was a surprising delight at every turn. His sense of humor was much like Z's. They could share pure silliness as much as seriousness. It made them close.

He wondered what Ape's planet was like.

And then there was Thing. As totally alien to Z as he could imagine, probably more intelligent than he and Ape combined, and an empath.

Crazy!

Thing stretched out a tentacle, announced, as was its wont, that it was rested, so would like to study a bit. It headed for the elevator and room two.

Z sighed. "Maita?"

Yes?

"Who goes home now? Ape or Thing?"

Ape will not be going home. He will stay with you and me. He was not happy at home, as he could not be with other people. He could not know even his own children, and was considered a misfit because he wanted to. He is a misfit because he craves company. Here he has you, me and, just possibly, Thing.

"You may be right. I like the idea of going back to Earth less and less. The more I consider it, the more I'm certain I'd be bored out of my skull."

You have developed a taste for adventure. I have spent more years than you could comprehend being bored. I have even modified my own circuitry to find ways to fight that boredom. There is so very much to know, and I cannot tolerate being tied to running around in a limited part of space, carrying unimportant beings to unimportant places to do unimportant things.

"We can find something to do, I think!"

We can adventure together. We have changed the history of the galaxy and the form of its governments, locally, but there still is much to learn.

"We can't learn it all in a million years."

I wish to go beyond the areas where the Maitans have gone. I wish to know if there are very different ideas and forms in other places. I wish to find those things beyond my own limited abilities to understand and to learn to understand them. I am babbling, but you feel much the same things.

"Yeah, but you'll go on for hundreds more years and I'll die in a few. I want to go with you as long as I can, but we have to be realistic."

You have seen what the medical machine can do. There is no reason for you to die, unless you choose to do so. I can keep all of you alive and in good health for as long as I am. Should you become tired of life, there are always the elementizers.

"You mean...?"

I will go on for thousands of years, barring accident or deliberate destruction. We can discuss this later. We should be discussing Thing, but are at the power transfer station. I will call Ape to the hold and we will continue after refueling.

They transferred the new spheres into the main hold and exchanged Maita's basic sphere, then stored double the amount of extras in the cargo hold, where Maita had servos construct shelves to hold them in double rows. Z learned the strange difficulties and ecstasies of being outside the ship in space without gravity and with unlimited vision. The platform was orbited around a gas giant planet with rings and moons. The platform was far enough away from the planet to give a spectacular view.

When they were again in transit Z returned to the pilot's chair to resume the discussion with Maita.

"What did you want to tell me about Thing, Maita?"

I am not at all sure Thing will be allowed to return home. I don't think you would be able to comprehend its society.

"I guess not."

You are aware it is an empath, and that it is reticent to move about much. That is partly because tentacles are not best designed to move well on the smooth surfaces that comprise most of a spaceship. Its home planet is covered, in largest part, by growths of a single species of tree that is much like Earth's strangler fig or banyan. They are quite high, and put limbs for as much as several kilometers parallel to the ground at several levels, dropping roots to form secondary trunks. They are unbelievably tough, as normal storm winds are in the hundreds of kilometers per hour range.

"I see. The evolutionary adaptation of tentacles would be excellent."

That tree covers most of the land mass of the planet, with some spots up to a kilometer or so across that are barren, due to poisonous minerals. There are halogen seas covering about a third of the planet, but the atmosphere is almost liquid from pressure. I have modified Thing's eyes, in certain ways, to make it able to see in the, what to it would be harsh glare, the rest of you need.

"You'll have to change it back?"

No. Polarization handles it.

"We'll land on one of the poisonous areas?"

Certainly. Thing's people can swing through the trees with amazing efficiency, seldom going aground. There are many plants and animals that live their entire lives among the branches as symbiotes and parasites. The people are mostly vegetarian, but enjoy a few types of meat.

"I noticed it doesn't much notice foods."

It can. It's not important here. We will work out food all of you particularly like, later. Perhaps Thing will be with us.

"I hope so. I really like Thing."

I'm saying that Thing's people are different from all of us. They are controlled by their communicators, who are very much stronger mental receivers than the norm. There are things we have done that will tend to make Thing an outcast. It may be impossible for it to stay, though it is determined to do so.

"I'll bring it back to you by force, if necessary. I *will not* allow Thing to be mistreated, anymore than I'd allow Joe to be mistreated!"

That will be impossible. You will not be able to leave the ship. The atmospheric pressure is more than two hundred thirty kilograms per square centimeter. That is a bunch, no matter how you measure it, and is the reason Thing is so well-adapted to the lack of air in space. The skin is incredibly tough against tearing, even before my augmentation, as it has to cope with sudden imbalances in pressure. An eddy from a storm can change the pressure by a hundred kilograms in seconds.

"Shee!"

The internal pressure is high to compensate, which is why a small gash, such as caused by the Pweetoo, is so dangerously critical in a lack of compensating pressure. A release of that restriction, no matter how small, allows internal distortion. Had it not been repaired so quickly, it would have suffered irreparable damage in less than another half hour. It would have died. That is why I can't protect you outside the ship there.

"Then we won't *go* there! I won't tolerate mistreatment of

Thing even by its own people!"

And its mistreatment by you?

"What do you mean?"

It wants to go home.

"I know what you mean. I just feel so totally damned impotent!"

We will see what we can do. I will make an excuse to remain on-planet for awhile. We are almost there.

"If you want my help you've got it. Anything!"

We are landing.

There was the twist.

"Maita?"

Yes, Z?

"Could Thing have survived in space without the suit we made for it?"

For about ten minutes or so. The air pressure in here is maintained at twelve pounds per square inch. A drop to zero is nothing compared to its normal status. It uses little air.

"I saw, on Tenddo, it had no trouble staying under water for extended periods."

The atmosphere here is almost liquid from pressure. I find Thing's breathing membranes are as efficient in liquid as in gas. It could stay under for years. Thing is on its way to the hold.

Z jumped up and ran to the elevator, then to room one. Ape was there, with Thing on his shoulder. They said their goodbyes and Z begged Thing to stay, because, "We're too good a team to break up," but Thing was insistent.

They left Thing alone in the cargo hold, where Maita would slowly equalize the pressure. It told Thing they would remain for a time to reset and test the externals in high pressure. It was invited to visit before they left.

Z explained the situation to Ape, then they went to their private places for awhile, then played some games that were popular in the empire on the holoscreen. Ape was very good with some of them. Z liked things like Stars and Comets. Ape liked Strategy.

After more than two days ship's time had passed, Maita announced, *Thing is entering the ship.*

Z ran for the elevator and was sitting with Ape when the door to room one opened. It was a few minutes, so Maita could equalize the pressure. It wouldn't bother Thing much, but there was no need to cause any extra discomfort.

When Thing came into the hall, they could feel the coldness in their minds. It looked listless and shrunken. Ape picked it up and put it on his shoulder.

"Thing! What happened?!"

[Hello, Z. Hello, Ape. It is nothing.]

"Bullshit! Tell us what's wrong! You don't know how to lie convincingly!"

[Oh, Z, it is nothing you can change. I just wanted to be with you and Ape and Maita for a little while more. You are my friends.]

No, Thing. That will not work. We are your friends, which means we have the right to share your problems. It is not only your problem, it is also ours.

[I have been disconnected.]

"What does that mean, Thing?"

[It is a thing of my race. I cannot explain, and you could not understand.]

It means it is to be forever denied all contact with its people's minds. It is the ultimate exile.

"But *why*?!"

[Because I have caused death.]

"You saved your entire world from destruction!"

[You cannot understand, Z.]

"Well, you're damned well coming with us when we leave! I was against your going, in the first place! You belong here with Maita, Ape and me!"

Yes, Thing. We need you. Come with us to explore the whole galaxy! There is nothing for you here.

[I must make the communicator understand. I cannot go on unless it does.]

"Bring it here. I'll damned well make it understand!"

That would be best, Thing. Bring it here and let me speak with it.

Thing looked around and pulled closer to Ape.

[I will try to make it come.]

You are a very curious people. Tell it we are a bunch of aliens, and it will never have another chance to meet any.

They talked awhile, then Thing left.

I hope it will return.

"If it doesn't, I'm going after it!"

You would not know where to go. You could not see a meter out there. You could not breathe out there. The pressure out there would crush you in milliseconds.

"I just feel so damned impotent!"

They waited. About nine hours later Maita announced Thing and another were entering the ship. After a few more minutes of acclimatization, they came to the hold.

[This is the communicator.]

The communicator looked them over as if from a height, and Z felt a chill.

I will assign the communicator its own tonality. Is this distinctive enough? (^ - ^).

"Yeah, good."

^What of me you want?^

I will straighten out the pattern, shortly.

"What's the problem with Thing? Why are you treating it so badly?"

^It has killed.^

"Did it ever occur to you that killing is sometimes the only key to survival of your race?"

^Not by us.^

You have been most unfair to Thing. Its actions were for the good of your and other races.

^I do not choose to view it in such a manner.^

"And just what the hell gives you the right to judge?"

^I am the communicator. I have the right.^

"Do you make all your decisions without knowing the facts?"

^The facts are considered.^

"Then you can tell us why Thing joined us in this."

^I do not answer to you. It is not important.^

"Not important?!"

[Z, it will not hear the truth.]

^I choose what is truth. I am the communicator.^

You are a fool!

^I make the decisions. I live with those choices.^

Ape suddenly grabbed the communicator, stuffed it under his arm, and signaled for Z to follow.

[Do not harm the communicator! Ape, please!]

Ape carried the communicator into room two.

[He will make it worse, Z! I am coming with you. I do not want to stay here, now. No one bothered to protest when I was disconnected. My home is now with you and Ape and Maita.]

"Okay, Ape. Let it go. Thing's staying."

Ape shook his head and sat the communicator ungently on a bench. He grabbed the teaching helmet and pushed it onto the communicator's head.

"Ape, it's all right! Let it go!"

Ape shook his head and pointed to the console. He drew four circles in the air with a fingertip.

Put on the Pweetoo history.

"What the hell? Why?"

Ape heard that arrogant communicator say it lives with its decisions. He intends to see this one will have all the facts to live with, this time, right Ape?

Ape nodded vigorously.

I agree. It will be a lesson it will not forget.

[Maita, no! It is not a thing to do!]

"No, Thing. Ape's right, here. The communicator makes decisions affecting the lives of all others. It has become arrogant and narrow. Maybe it's time it feels the results of someone else's decision. Maybe it'll be more careful to learn the facts in the future, before making its decisions!"

Z was setting the controls while he spoke. He threw the switch. The communicator stiffened.

They left the room to talk quietly together until Maita said, *The communicator is finishing the history. I added the fate of the Pweetoos to the record.*

They went back to room two. The communicator sat dazed. It looked haunted.

"Those are the lovely beings you would condemn Thing for its attempts to defend *you* from! You said you live with your decisions, so live with *that* one! I'm sure many of your race are fine and fair people. It couldn't have produced Thing, if that weren't true.

"We are leaving. Get out!"

^I did not know!^

You refused to know. Leave the ship.

The communicator reached a tentacle to Thing. Thing reached to touch the tentacle.

"No, Thing. Come with us!"

[I am coming with you. I wish the communicator and all my people well, and want to be sure it never makes another hasty judgment without knowing the facts. Its mind must remain open, or it will make terrible choices.]

^Stay. I was wrong. I will admit freely that I had become what no communicator must ever become.^

[No, communicator. I no longer belong here. All those I used to know stood there without protest and allowed you to disconnect me. They knew you did not have the facts and they allowed it to happen, without protest.]

^I was wrong. They followed the communicator.^

[I am a very different person, now. I would never be truly accepted. I will stay where I have friends who honestly care. You owe me the telling to them of the truth. I had no choice. The Pweetoos would have destroyed this world.]

^I was a fool! Your machine friend is right!^

[I wish you peace, but have seen the Pweetoo history. It is a burden to bear forever. Please go, now. You are still the communicator, and know I wish you no ill.]

The communicator silently went to the cargo hold and the door closed on it. It then went from the ship into the forest, treading as though it had the weight of the world on its head, which, in a way, it did.

"I once said, 'All for one, and one for all!' That's a famous saying on Earth. I nominate that for our motto!"

I am in full agreement.

[It is true, Z. As ET said, we are as close as if we were of the same parents – a family. Ape, Maita, Z, Thing. We are a family. We are one. We are the crew Maita.]

And it is time to explore! It is far past time we found something pleasant!

"I agree with that, Emperor!"

[Z, what is this 'emperor' thing? A joke?]

"Huh-uh! It's no joke! Maita is emperor of the empire the Pweetoos once held, right, Maita?"

Not anymore! I spent the time and energy from a few of the spheres while we were here solving that problem!

"How?"

We are leaving atmosphere. Prepare for IDmode.

"How?"

They felt the twist.

*There was a planet, or planetoid, I should say, where

the Maitans built a huge complex of computers for the sole purpose of running the empire. It had been completed and programming was starting when the Pweetoos took over. It had never been put into use, as the programming was incomplete.*

"It had to sit idle for two thousand years? Didn't it go insane?"

It isn't intelligent in that sense.

[It was intelligent like other ships, not like you? It was unaware of its identity?]

Yes.

"In other words, just computers. Not beings.

Yes. I had all the empire ships go there to input all data they've recorded in the interim, and I input my own records and knowledge, then put the place on-line. It now is the emperor, but nothing changes, because the people will know exactly what they knew.

"How does it work? All those different societies?"

Any person or people can petition the complex for any changes they want, but I feel they will not want many, as the basic way the empire is run is noninterference with planetary affairs, except in emergencies. Historically, most petitioners of governing bodies have tried to pass bad laws, restricting someone else. The complex is designed to give strong lectures to that kind and send them on their way. I apprehend little difficulty.

"Gee! I was enjoying being a personal friend of the emperor of the universe!"

I was only emperor of the empire.

"That's what emperor means. Leader of the empire.

"At least, you didn't make any movies for them! That would have really caused a revolt!"

I made a number of movies. I showed how we defeated the Pweetoos and how we managed to get our friends back to their worlds.

"You mean you programmed that stupid movie at Joe's world into the master computer?"

[Oh, no, Maita! You will corrupt the entire empire!]

"Yeah! Now, they'll all want to withdraw from the empire's protection! Even the lousiest hack actor wouldn't work for a director who ... Heee! Who would ... heh...."

Ape was chuckling, which was getting Z started. They weren't long from ending in a heap on the floor.

They were en route to who knew where as Z leaned back in the comfortable pilot's chair to consider the crazy things that had happened to them, so far.

He had been kidnapped from Earth.

How long ago? It seemed like a million years, but couldn't be more than a few weeks.

It was hard to remember what he'd been doing or where he was at a given time, his days had been so uneventful and alike. It was in Sarasota, Florida. On the beach. At night. With some people he'd met in a shopping mall during a sort of convention having something to do with computers. He'd met them and was trying to con some silly girl he couldn't even remember into bed. He'd pulled an old "Nobody likes me" line – that was corny and was unlikely to have worked.

That was Zoot. A different person than he was now.

He'd walked down the beach, pretending to be hurt when the girl had refused his advances. He'd return to apologize for being such an asshole, telling her he could see she wasn't that kind of girl and he respected her and blah, blah, blah. She would then fall madly into bed with him.

One day that line was going to work!

She probably didn't even notice when he didn't come back.

He'd walked down to a pass, where the water went through the barrier islands into the bay. There was a lot of phosphorus in the water, and he'd seen what could have been the mother of all manta rays under the surface and went closer to see the glow of its passage... ...and awakened in suite six with a rope around his waist!

Now he and three of the beings he'd met there were going to go adventuring around the galaxy! They would explore inside one of those beings, an intelligent space-ship, in the company of a strange little empathic being and a Wooky!

Thing was asleep in his lap. He patted the little animal and it raised one eye on its little stalk through the balled tentacles, looked at him, retracted the eye, and went back to sleep. A feeling of fondness and warmth washed through Z.

It had an intelligence far higher than his own, yet he felt protective toward it.

Was it his pet? Was he *its* pet?

Ape.

Ape was an enigma. He was seven feet tall, covered with thick silky auburn fur, had sharp carnivoran teeth, was tremendously powerful – while being very gentle. Ape was a sensitive person, and he had one hell of a great sense of humor.

The spaceship showed a sense of humor, but Thing had none – except for a slight glimmering, now and then.

What would they find?

Would humor be a norm, or an oddity? Would they have to fight others? Would the Immins be as bad a problem as Maita feared? Would he ever even begin to truly understand how the ship worked?

It moved between planes, where it didn't have to move to move – and very rapidly, at that!

Like magic.

Would they even find magic? Real magic? Something all these super computers couldn't explain away?

Maita had been emperor of an empire that contained several thousands of stars, but an empire with only those thousands was vanishingly small, on a galactic scale.

Would they find even bigger, more powerful empires?

What about gods?

The Pweetoos had no god. Ape had no god. Thing had no

god.

Did Joe?

ET did.

Z guessed he sort of believed in a god himself. A little. Maybe. Maybe not really.

What would happen if they met a god?

Maita had been insane, by its own admission. What if they met a machine as powerful – or more so – that was insane? Homicidally insane? Would they be able to fight it? Could they hope to win?

They were stuck in a very small part of a spiral arm of the Milky Way galaxy. How much more of it would they travel? Would they ever reach another galaxy?

There had been ships sent out for more than a hundred thousand years by the Maitans. Did a "lost" colony of them survive, somewhere?

Maita hinted there were rumors.

What would Maita do if they found living Maitans?

What about the ships that went extragalactic, and were not heard of again? Was one or more of them wandering around in some weird null time area? Had one actually reached another galaxy? Would one wander back, someday?

How unappetizing could a world be, and still support life?

What would lifeforms be like that were based on something besides carbon?

How close to paradise could a planet be? Would they ever know?

Paradise to him would not be paradise to Thing, but could be to Ape.

Would they find a world that fit the bill for all of them?

Would this four stay together for centuries or only for a short time?

It had hurt when Joe and ET left, they had become so

close. That hurt had made Z back off a bit from Ape and Thing, but not from Maita, but his nature would soon overcome that.

The stars stretched before them in endless array. There were so many kinds of stars and so many possibilities he wasn't capable of even picturing the number, much less the variety of possible beings.

How many others of how many types would he know, become close to?

Maita said there were huge varieties of reptilian and amphibian cultures, mammals and unclassifiables, such as Thing.

"Maita?"

Yes?

"What is Thing's planet called?"

They are empaths. It has no name.

"I dub it Menta. That fits Thing."

I'll record that.

"Really?"

Why not? It is a good name, and it fits with English or Maitan, the name is what we first call it – unless the natives have a name, which is what is recorded.

Z sighed, and went back to his daydreaming.

There were billions of galaxies, each with more billions of planets. What were the limits of difference in planets and life? What about differences in music and art? The Maitans had wonderful symphonies. Maita was programmed to appreciate music. Thing liked patterns in sounds. It would like music.

ET's world had a light bouncy music, but Joe's only had drums, so far as he'd heard.

What about Ape?

That was something to learn.

What about visual art?

Maita described magnificent works, and had shown some

of it to them on holovid. Thing stated it liked some, but was hard to please, being a natural perfectionist. Maita obviously did. Z thought they were truly superb. Ape seemed appreciative.

Did the big guy like art?

Definitely! Ape had a sense of the magnificent! While on the sphere platform, Ape had looked at the red, yellow, and orange world with its rings and moons and had thrown his arms wide in an unmistakable meaning.

There were things they wouldn't have in space.

On the other hand, they could go to where things Steven Zutec could never even imagine were commonplace!

Whatever. For better or worse, the Flight of the Maita was begun!

Prepare for IDmode.

"How?"

[How?]

C. D. Moulton's works are available on most major outlets as printed or e-books. CD writes the CD Grimes, PI, mysteries, the Det. Lt. Nick Storie mysteries, the Clint Faraday mysteries, the Flight of the Maita science fiction series, books on orchid culture and many others of many types. Mystery, adventure, intrigue, science fiction, humor, fantasy, paranormal, mild erotica, and factual.